Nightjar

(Sparrow Man Series)

Veil of Shadows

Book Five

M. R. Pritchard

Meg is a ticking time bomb. She's on edge after Sparrow tried to kill her. Now she's saddled with an amputee Angel and two refugees from the Earthen plane. King Gabriel is in prison. She also kidnapped baby Thrush. Can Meg figure out how to stop Thrush from turning into a Nightjar or will revenge win her focus?

Not Again

Skeele

"Christ," Skeele spit, followed by more swearing in Hellspeak as he bent to lift Meg from the ground. *Not again*, he thought. This can't be happening again. Skeele lifted Meg, one arm under her knees, another across her back.

The energy in the room went berserk. The new recruits were wild, shouting and shoving ensued. Duke and Chel did their best to calm them, but this was the kind of chaos that ensued when the throne was threatened. The throne of Hell was a coveted thing here. A shadowed realm where darkness reigned, the malevolence of the throne loomed, it had *presence*. Lucifer's throne steeped in sinister intentions, cunningly concealed beneath a shroud of deception woven by the very souls in subjugation. If Lucifer's rule was night, Meg's rule was day. She was a flicker of hope for the souls of Hell. Meg started to tame the veil; started to loosen the chains. The creatures of Hell would always require reining in, but for the first time in eons, the Hellions were doing it with minimal violence and death. It was paying off; the more souls a realm held, the greater the power.

Skeele lifted Meg, exhaling a breath of relief when he felt solid bones under her skin. It wasn't like last time. Last time he lifted her like this off the dusky grass of the backyard, it sounded like Rice Krispies crackling under her skin. He'd never heard nor felt the weight of someone with every bone in their body broken. She was nothing more than a sack of flesh that day and simply thinking about how she felt in his arms made his stomach twist.

Meg didn't remember, therefore ever since that day she never understood his need to protect her. She was hazardous to her own health ninety-nine percent of the time. Hellions didn't give a shit about much, but protecting their leader- they cared about that. They wanted to protect Meg because she was different. She gave them hope. Skeele never wanted to experience lifting her as a bag of bones again. Yet, here he was.

"Get them out," Skeele shouted to Tukka and Chel as he walked toward the bar. The energy of the room cooled as the other Hellions left.

Skeele dropped Meg's lifeless body on the bar and slapped her pale cheeks, trying to wake her. Blood leaked from wounds in her leg, arm, and stomach. The most concerning was the one over her heart. Gaping wide, he could see the slow pulse of her heart where her breastbone was pierced, and the skin torn back.

"I'll get the blood," Klaus shouted as he ran behind the bar, ripped open the fridge and tore out every bag of blood that was stocked there.

This wasn't medicine like on the Earthen plane. Heaven and Hell each had their own methods of saving a life. Too bad Skeele wasn't skilled at any of them—none of the Hellions were. They needed something more, but battlefield survival would have to do. Blood cured much. Skeele scanned Meg's injuries... he wasn't sure blood would cure this.

Skeele and Tukka tore open the bags of blood and dripped them into Meg's mouth. The wounds seeped, their flow never seeming to stop. Rivulets of viscous blood ran over pale skin and torn clothing.

"Wake up," Skeele spit from clenched teeth.

Nothing happened. Meg didn't swallow. The blood simply pooled in her mouth. She was barely breathing and Skeele was so worked up he didn't trust his eyes. Her breaths were shallow. He blinked. Was she even breathing?

"Pour it in the wounds," Tukka suggested.

"Can't hurt," Skeele said as he opened a fresh bag of blood and poured it over the stab wounds on Meg's chest and stomach.

Tukka ripped open another bag using his teeth and poured blood into the wounds on her arm and leg.

They waited.

Nothing happened.

Meg's breathing slowed. Each breath was further apart. Her head tipped to the side with the pressure of Tukka's fingers as he felt for a pulse, worry creasing his dark skin. Tukka shook his head. "It's barely, anything. This is not good."

The blood that pooled in her mouth slowly dripped down a pale cheek and pooled along the valleys of delicate ear. Meg looked worse than before. Worse than ever. She looked dead.

"I'm going to get help," Skeele said, running for the door. "Don't let anyone in here!"

A SPEC OF GRACE

Jed and Shay

Someone was pounding on the door. Jed and Shay made eye contact from across the room, then both looked at the sleeping baby.

"Make it stop," Shay said. "It's going to wake him."

Jed and Shay weren't parents, but they were playing the part, and sleep deprivation was straining their relationship. He had spent his whole life in the run, now he was a sitting duck and responsible for two lives.

Jed clutched a knife. Not just any knife, a small switchblade that he'd carved with runes and coated in magic. It wouldn't save them, but it would gain them some time if he had to use it. It would delay whatever onslaught came for them until help arrived.

Jed opened the door just a crack.

There was a Hellion there, the one Meg called Skeele. He was anxious, pacing, and–more concerning–covered in blood.

"Meg needs help," Skeele growled.

"What kind of help?" Jed asked, gripping the knife tighter in his hand.

"The life or death kind."

Jed stilled. "Sounds like Meg." He didn't trust the hulking demon, afraid that the Hellion might try to blast through the door and get the baby that Meg made Jed and Shay swear on their lives to protect and hide.

Skeele's arms went wide, "Are you coming?" he shouted.

Jed slammed the door closed and turned to face Shay.

"What?" Shay asked.

"I think something bad has happened," Jed said as he crossed the room to get his bag. "I have to go." Jed knew whatever happened, wasn't good.

"You can't," Shay's eyes were wide as she stood, reaching for him. "Don't leave us."

Shay knew how to survive the apocalypse of the Earthen plane, but Hell? Hell was a different matter. For both of them. She'd never been here before. He'd never been here before. He'd taught her as much as he could about the spells and runes over the days I had locked them in this room. But he had to go now. Because if something happened to Meg, they were shit out of luck.

"Tell Noah as soon as he gets back," Jed said, concern overtaking his voice. "Noah will know what to do."

Shay nodded, blue hair falling over her eyes.

"I'll come back as soon as I can," he promised, stepping closer and gripping her arm. "I'll be back."

Shay nodded but worry glazed her eyes.

Jed backed out the door, checking the runes along the floor and around the door lock to make sure they were intact. He locked the door and turned to find the Hellion.

Skeele was pacing, cracking his knuckles, and looking thoroughly on edge.

"What happened?" Jed asked.

Skeele didn't answer, instead he grabbed Jed by the collar of his jacket and ran for the stairwell. Skeele ran down four steps at a time dragging Jed along. Jed tripped and stumbled, slamming his knee against the wall as he caught his footing.

"Let go of me you asshat," Jed shouted, arms flailing as I dragged him through the air on the descent. "You're going to break my fucking neck."

Skeele let go. "We need to move fast." He kept running down the stairs, the sound of heavy boots echoing off stone.

Jed followed, shaking off nerves. He didn't know what he was about to walk into. But if Meg was in the room, that usually meant he'd be walking into a shit show.

Skeele led Jed to a Hellion-marked door on the first floor. He pushed the door open and dragged Jed by the arm of his jacket. Slower this time.

The metallic scent of blood was thick in the air. It only took seconds for Jed to see where it was coming from. There was a body on the bar, and it looked pretty lifeless.

"Come on," Skeele urged as he crossed the room.

As Jed approached the bar, a hand flew to his mouth. Shit. This was not good. Meg was dead. That meant he'd probably be dead soon. And so would Shay. And so would that baby.

"We need your help," Skeele said, rounding the bar.

Jed threw his hands in the air. "How can I help you with this?" Hands went to his hair and tugged. His life was over. Shay's life was over. And God only knows what would happen to the baby upstairs. The portals were gone, and Jed couldn't transverse the realms like Meg.

"Do something," the dark Hellion in the room begged. His eyes wide and black. "She's going to die soon."

Skeele was pacing and growling and muttering in Hellspeak.

"I can't bring dead people back to life," Jed said, he didn't deal in death magic. "That's a different type of–"

Skeele crossed the room and ripped Jed's backpack off. "You know magic." He pointed at the tattooed runes on Jed's arms. "You know spells. You must know something that can help."

"Are you sure she's dead?" Jed asked.

Tukka checked her pulse again. "It's faint. Very faint." The large Hellion touched Meg's hair, leaving bloody fingerprints on her forehead.

The Hellions were savage creatures and as far as Jed knew, they didn't care about much. But it appeared they cared very much for this lifeless person. If only Meg knew.

Jed took his bag from Skeele's hands and poured it out on the portion of the bar that wasn't covered in blood. There were vials, papers, bags of sand, bags of bones, and other strange little trinkets. Jed was looking for the book. He sorted everything until he found it. The book was really nothing more than a palm sized sketchpad, but it was ages old and fell into his possession after meeting another Nephilim years ago. He flipped through the pages, searching. Searching for something. Anything that could help.

"Come on!" Skeele pounded his fists on the bar. Empty glasses clanged together; the pings of glass threatening to shatter added to the angst in the room.

"I'm looking." Jed's fingers danced over the stained pages, his eyes scanned in rapid movements. "Ok. Ok. I think I found something that might help."

Jed went to work. He marked the wooden bar around

Meg's body with charcoal, sprinkled sand, and arranged small bones near her head and feet. Last, he chose a small jar of white liquid that luminated faintly.

"What's that?" Skeele asked with a growl.

"Do you know?" Jed asked, one brow raised. "Some call it grace. Or at least, that's what I was told." He tilted the vial and the liquid inside luminated brighter.

"How'd you get that?" Skeele asked, eyes narrowed on the vial.

"I inherited it." Jed flipped the cap and stared at the two Hellions. "Now I need you both to shut up or join in."

Jed chanted ancient words from the book. The runes of sand glowed, the bones rattled like a rattlesnake tail. He tipped the vial onto his finger and pressed it to Meg's forehead. Chanting more, the words that originally sounded off and hard to wrap his tongue around became fluid and easier to annunciate the more he repeated them. The spec of grace on Meg's forehead pulsed. Jed was backlit in blue light as he motioned for Skeele and Tukka to join in.

The two Hellions made eye contact in apprehension but finally joined and repeated Jed's words.

Meg took a single breath. Her wounds oozed. Congealed blood dipped and formed circular crests. The spec of grace on her forehead glowed brighter.

Hope rose in Jed's chest. It was working. It was working!

Suddenly, Meg's wounds began gushing blood. Rivers flowed out of her. More blood than the Hellions had given her. Blood spilled onto the floor and the speck of grace turned from white to black. Meg's forehead smoked. Her body shuddered. The smell was putrid as the smoke billowed toward the ceiling.

"No," Skeele stopped chanting. "What did you do?" He

grabbed a rag from the counter behind him and wiped the dot of grace off her forehead.

"What the hell," Jed shouted. "You broke the spell."

"You were killing her," Skeele growled. "And now I'm going to kill you!"

IDLED WITH DESPAIR

Teari sat on the edge of her bed. There was no balcony in her room. No extra furnishings. There were plenty of clothes and a variety of prosthetic limbs Noah had brought her to try. She stared at her arms; the nub at the wrist, the nub at the elbow. Nothing had prepared her for this. Not the decades of training with the Legion or the decades of being King Gabriel's personal healer. It was rare for an Angel to lose a limb for good. They always grew back. Teari had some practice with that magic. But now, human blood pumped through her veins. It had altered her, stopped her powers. She'd told Meg they would come back but to be completely honest, Teari wasn't sure. And the thought of being limbless for the rest of her time was too much to handle.

Teari was trapped within a desolate chamber of despair. Surrounding her were frigid walls that echoed with the silence of abandonment. The air hung heavy with oppressive darkness, suffocating any flicker of hope that dared to linger. Teari had once soared among the Seven Kingdoms of Heaven, a radiant beacon of grace, her purpose to heal and protect. Now, her wings weighed heavy with the burden of her own suffering, rendered powerless by the loss of her hands. Tears streaked down her ashen cheeks, the remnants of a shattered spirit. Every breath was a struggle as if the very air had turned against her. Her wounds throbbed, a constant reminder of the Fast-Zombie War. Although, from her hospital bed on the Earthen plane, she hadn't seen the worst of it.

Teari glanced at the four walls of her room. There was no window. And she was sure she knew why Meg hadn't given her a window. The urge to jump out it and plunge to the rocks below was strong. Or... maybe it was glamour. Teari stood and walked toward the exterior wall. She rubbed her arms across the green plaster searching for something, anything. Perhaps something hidden that she couldn't see with the naked eye. She'd take any way out she could find. Teari stood on her toes, crouched on the ground, pressed her cheek to the walls, and inspected every inch of the room. She shoved the bed away from the wall with her shoulder and kept going.

"Let me out," Teari whispered. Something was surging in her chest, a feeling of panic she'd never felt before. She tore through the room, looking for an escape. She shoved and kicked, she tipped over the nightstand, shoved the small bed aside. The scabbed scars on her arms opened and oozed blood and serous fluid.

Is this how Meg and Nightingale felt all those times they'd been locked up? Empty and cold? Sad and lonely? Pissed off and hating the world?

Maybe Nightingale could help her. Night frequented the Astral plane but the only way for Teari to get there was to sleep. She lay on the floor, in the far corner, hidden by the disheveled room, and closed her eyes.

Soul Searching

Noah

"She was already dead," Jed shouted. "I didn't kill her, you all did!" He pointed at Skeele and Tukka.

Skeele ran around the bar, headed for Jed. "I didn't kill her," he growled. "I'd never kill her."

"Who killed what?" Noah's voice pierced the room. He appeared in front of Jed. Protectively. "You won't kill my man, Jeddio."

Skeele paused as best he could. It was hard to stop the killing motion of a Hellion, but he managed. Then he pointed to the bar. "Meg," was all Skeele said.

If a ghost could pale, Noah did. "No. No no no no no." He ran toward Meg. "What happened?"

"She just poofed into the room at my feet all stabbed up," Skeele said. "We tried blood. Jed used some bullshit spell that burned her face."

"She took a breath!" Jed thrust his hands toward Meg's body. "You saw it! We all saw it. The spell was working."

"It was not working," Skeele shouted back, muscles tense.

Noah held up his hands. "Just shut up. Both of you." He touched Meg's face, brushing off the burnt skin. If she's dead or in between, she might be in the Astral. Noah placed both palms on each side of Meg's head and closed his eyes. His image wavered as he searched the Astral plane for Meg. If she were there, it might mean they could get her back into her body.

Noah searched. He searched and searched and searched. He looked between every shadow of the void of the Astral but found nothing. The Astral was infinite, but there were places that he and Nightingale had created. Places that a wandering Meg might find familiar. He searched for them. A red tree by a stream. A kaleidoscope of stars above a hilltop. A hot tub at the top of a snowy mountain. Each place he visited tore at his gut. The memories of Nightingale were strong, and even stronger was the knowledge that he'd never get to spend time with her here again. Noah tried to push thoughts of Nightingale out of his mind. But memories are a spiral of emotion. It was a battle Noah barely won.

He felt a coldness surround him. A familiar coldness. Clea was nearby. Noah scanned the Astral shouting for Meg one last time. There was nothing. He had to go back. He had to go face Clea and tell her that Meg was nowhere to be found.

———

"Oh child," Clea's voice was full of sorrow. Her ruby red lips pinched together. Everyone stared at her. "It seems this curse is familial. We lose children too often here."

Clea knew about loss. Lucifer had lost Clea then Clea had lost Meg to the Earthen plane in an attempt to save her. Meg had lost her own child before it had ever been born. Clea and Megs reunion was bound to be ended soon enough. It was all a vicious circle in this bloodline. Clea could see some of the future, with visions and omens, nothing she'd seen ever ended well.

"We have to do something," Noah said, moving his hands away from Meg's head. He didn't know what to say. At least Meg was here. At least they didn't have to search for her bones like Gabriel searched for twenty-five years for Clea's. Noah knew the story. At least they had a tiny bit of closure, seeing her here, like this.

"Have you tried everything to save her?" Clea asked, her image wavering, nearly transparent.

"We tried blood," Skeele said.

"I had a spell and some Angel grace," Jed began collecting his items and placing them in his backpack.

"Angel grace?" Noah asked.

Jed nodded. "It didn't work." He pinched the vial between his fingers and held it up to the light before placing it in his bag.

Angel grace might not have worked, but they had an actual Angel in the castle.

"I'll be right back," Noah said, just before he disappeared. "Don't touch her," his voice echoed throughout the Hellion lair.

Love, Death, and Antidepressants

Teari

Forcing oneself to dream is never easy. Teari wasn't sure how long she lay on the floor; there wasn't sunlight drifting across a window to give her an estimate of the passing time, there were no clocks, she heard no footsteps in the hallway outside her door. Her eyes felt gritty and her eyelids restless. Her body didn't want to sleep, and her mind was a flurry of coercive thoughts as she tried her best to convince herself that she was tired. When she finally drifted off to sleep, her dreams were nightmares–they had been since she lost her hands. The fast-zombies forever chased her. Their snapping jaws and gnarled teeth threatened to bite the few limbs she had left. Sparrow was there and he was nothing she remembered. He bit her over and over again. He didn't hold back; he didn't recognize her as the healer and Legion guard who had fought by his side, who had once desired him. Nightingale didn't save her. She didn't show up and interrupt the nightmares like she used to. There was only radio silence from the Astral.

Teari woke a few hours later. Her shoulders ached, her wings ached, and her wounds had scabbed over again leaving a crust over the incision scars where the doctors on the Earthen plane had done their best to stitch her back together. It wasn't their fault that her arms looked like Frankenstein. They were doing the best they could. She didn't forget that if the group of them hadn't encountered the National Guard in Pennsylvania, she'd surely be dead, and her soul lost. Teari forced herself to thank her lucky stars every day, but it felt like a lie. She didn't feel lucky and most days, she'd wished she'd just died on the Earthen plane instead of living like this.

A single tear slid down her cheek. If Nightingale wasn't in the Astral, where was she? Teari knew she'd been gone from the Seven Kingdoms of Heaven for weeks. Without a word and unable to reach Gabriel or anyone else, she was certain Nightingale would come looking for answers in her dreams. But she didn't. And Teari wasn't sure what that meant.

Meg was keeping something from her. They all were.

"Teari?" a familiar voice asked.

She didn't hear a door open so it could only be Noah. He was a thing of the Astral but tethered to Meg's soul by lifelong friendship and sacrifice. It was hard to remember with his boyish good looks and habit for pranks and dirty jokes.

"What?" Teari asked from the cover she currently occupied, unmoving; not giving Noah an idea of where she was.

"I need your help." Furniture scraped across the tile floor as he followed her voice. "What the heck happened in here? It's a mess."

"Nothing." Teari rolled onto her back and stared at the

ceiling. She blew a small white feather off her face. "Can you just go away?"

"Nope." Noah appeared over Teari. "We got a problem downstairs. The biggest of problems."

"Meg ordered me not to leave this room," Teari reminded him. "So I'm going to stay here." Teari rested her forearms on her head but moved them immediately. It was hard to get comfortable in any position.

"Yeah, about that," he reached down and grabbed Teari's upper arms, tugging her to stand. "You want one of the prosthetics?"

"I'm not going anywhere," Teari said as she stood. Her body was limp, lacking muscle tone like a doll.

Noah was already opening her door.

"I don't like the prosthetics." She waved her arms. "They're uncomfortable."

"Then leave them. Come on." Noah tugged at her shirt. "Meg's in trouble."

"Meg's always in trouble," Teari mumbled.

"You're not wrong." Noah swung the door open and dragged Teari into the hallway. "But right now she's dying, and we need help."

"How much dying?" Teari added air quotes when she said dying. Meg was always in some kind of trouble, her life always teetering on the edge of an early death. Not much surprised Teari anymore when it came to Meg.

It annoyed Noah when he shouted, "She's bleeding out in the Hellion lair! I could see her heart." He paused. "I mean, at least I know she has a heart now." His eyebrows rose in realization.

"Shit," Teari ran out the door, disoriented in the dark hallways of the castle and began running in the wrong direction. Noah righted her with a hard pull in the correct direction and led her down the stairwell and hallways to the lair.

Noah and Teari burst through the door of the lair. Teari ran to Meg's side. It didn't look good. It didn't look good at all. The air dripped with a metallic odor. There was so much blood. And the remnants of a spell. Teari brushed the sand away and destroyed the runes surrounding Meg's body.

Jed shouted in protest, but no one paid attention to what he was saying.

Skeele filled her in on what they'd tried. "Can you do something?" he asked.

Teari rested her arm on Meg's chest, searching for a sign of life. "I can't do what I used to." She bit her lip, wishing she had hands. After all her years of healing, she had never felt so useless. She couldn't do a thing without her healing magic.

"Have you tried giving her fresh blood?" Teari asked.

Skeele's back went straight. Teari would have to be blind to miss his reaction.

"Did she fix Sparrow?" Teari asked. "His blood would be the best option. They have a bond."

"Sparrow is gone," Skeele said. "He's out of the picture."

Teari frowned. "Gone?"

Skeele motioned to the sky. "I'm assuming he went home."

"Crap." Teari stepped away from the bar and paced for a moment. She looked at everyone, studying them. Jed wouldn't do. Even with his mixed heritage, Tukka was unhinged at the moment. Her eyes paused on Skeele, the only one in the room who was semi-calm, but Teari could tell under his skin he was ready to lose it. The worry on his face was different; deeper than the worry of a bystander.

"What are you?" she asked, looking at Skeele. She waved her nubbed arms in a flurry. "Who are you to her? There's a reason you're so upset that she's dying right now. There's something between you two?"

He cleared his throat and reset his demeanor. "Hellion First Command."

Teari knew the First Command was the closest to the leader of Hell. There was a bond. Duty and sacrifice demanded it. Even if Meg and Skeele never admitted it to each other. No matter how weak the bond might be, it would work the best. Without Sparrow, Meg was only tethered to Noah, and being a spirit of the Astral, he didn't have blood.

"Your blood will do." Teari pointed at him with the nub of her right arm. "Give her your blood. Right now. Before she's gone forever."

Blood Letting

Skeele

He knew what fresh blood would do to Meg. The lust, the lack of control. He'd seen it at the Vermont cabin. It wasn't safe to give her fresh blood with everyone watching. People talked and it was bad enough she didn't have wings; that fact brought enough rumors. He didn't trust those in this room not to spread the image of Meg high on fresh blood. The new recruits were probably already spreading rumors. Skeele knew they'd reach the Deacons soon, and they'd start meddling.

Skeele knew it was Sparrow who did this. Meg wouldn't get close enough to anyone else. She was dangerous to herself and others, but she kept her distance. She always kept her distance. There was a time when Skeele respected Sparrow, learned from him, grew into the Hellion he was today. But Skeele swore on the throne of Hell that he'd kill Sparrow if he ever saw him again. It was the only right thing to do. Sparrow deserved nothing more than death after what he'd done to Meg. She hated the Hellions, but she forgot

Sparrow was one of them. That or she did her best to ignore it. He wasn't so special.

Skeele carried Meg out of the Hellion lair. She weighed nothing, a feather in his arms. The others didn't follow. They saw the time he spent with her during the months following her fall from the sky. It was Meg's room, but he had a space to sit and watch and protect. He had a chair that no one else sat in. But he never thought he'd be returning to it so quickly.

Skeele took Meg to her bedroom. He kicked open the door, entered, and set her gently on the bed. He turned and grabbed the chair Meg had used many times to lock him and the other Hellions out. He closed the door, locked it, and propped the chair against the handle. He couldn't risk anyone coming in to see this. And if she didn't make it, he wasn't sure he'd be leaving the room at all. It was his duty to protect and serve her throne. Yet, here she was, dead as a doornail under his watch. There was no going back if he couldn't fix this.

Skeele grabbed his blade from the holster at his thigh. As he walked, he held his right arm up and sliced across the soft, inner skin. Blood came quickly. He kneeled and held his bleeding wrist over Meg's mouth.

"Please work," he begged with a whisper. *She isn't supposed to die here*, he reminded himself.

Blood pooled in her mouth. Skeele felt stiff lips on his skin, but it wasn't like before; there was no firm tone to her lips, no draw from her mouth. No aggressive sucking, moans in her throat, or eyelids twitching in haste. None of that. She was simply there as he bled into her.

When the drops stopped, he pulled away. The blood slowly disappeared down her throat. Skeele felt a spec of hope since it didn't pour down her chin, wasted like the bagged blood in the lair. His gaze scanned her closely, waiting. Finally, he moved away from the bed, took the club chair from the far side of the room, and dragged it closer. He sat, elbows on his knees, fingers threaded together in worry. He waited.

———

Meg's chest rose. It was faint but visible in the fading light of Hellsky. Skeele moved closer. He pressed two fingers to her neck and felt a faint pulse. He grabbed his blade, sliced his wrist again, and rested it over her mouth. She didn't move. Didn't suck. But, her skin changed from pale deathly white to the slightest tinge of pink. When the blood stopped dripping, he licked the cut to close it.

Skeele examined her wounds. He'd been afraid to move her much when he carried her back to the room, but now that there were signs of life, he needed to care for her. He moved her limp arms out of her leather jacket, her head flopping to the side as he turned her. He ran his finger over the stab wound on her arm. It still looked fresh, but it wasn't dripping or oozing like before. It was healing. Next, he ripped the neck of Meg's shirt all the way to the bottom hem and pushed the fabric aside. He inspected the stab wounds to her stomach, his hand smoothing over the skin of her abdomen. They were gone. Just soft, delicate skin with a spattering of tattoos. Skeele's eyes moved to the wound over her heart. It was deep still. He could see the splintered bone; the red flesh of her heart was stitching itself together. The tattoo of the sparrow in flight was torn. *Good*, he thought. He wanted to cut off that tattoo. The torn skin through the center of it wasn't enough. He never wanted to see or hear the word Sparrow again. It didn't deserve to be on her skin in any form.

Skeele glanced down her legs. There was more blood. He unbuttoned Meg's leather pants and dragged them down. One large gash to her thigh was bright red and glistening, longer than his hand. If he knew anything, that must've hurt like a bitch.

Skeele collected the bloody clothes and threw them in the corner. He went to her bathroom to find towels and soap before setting them on the countertop and starting the tub. He couldn't let her sit in blood. It was bad enough that she'd sat in it for this long.

He did his best to move her gently off the bed. He slid one arm under her shoulders, another under her knees. Congealed blood spread across his arms. If Meg knew what was happening, she didn't let him know. Her eyes were still closed, her breaths were just as shallow as when he watched her take the last one in the Hellion lair. Skeele grabbed a washcloth and wiped the dirt and blood off Meg's face. He dampened her hair before grabbing shampoo from the shower and massaging it into the blood-soaked strands. He used the washcloth to rub the crusted blood off her shoulder. His thick fingers smoothed over her inked skin. When he was done cleaning her skin and her wounds, the bathwater was red. He drained it and refilled the tub with fresh water to rinse her.

Skeele changed the bloody sheets on the bed and searched for clothing from the closet. It was all jeans and leather and small. Skeele left the closet and went to the club chair he'd sat in for so many weeks waiting for her to heal the last time. He pulled the chair away from the wall and grabbed the leather bag that was shoved behind it. He'd needed clean clothes before when he refused to leave her side. Noah had brought him random clothing from his quarters. He chose a large button-down flannel. It wasn't what Meg typically wore but it was clean, and it would keep her warm and give him easy access to her wounds. He dried her and moved her to the bed, then dressed her in his giant shirt.

After, Skeele sat on the chair, his large hands gripping the armrests and he hated being here again. Watching, waiting, praying that she'd wake up. At least she wouldn't wake covered in death. If she woke at all.

———

The days and nights went on. Skeele bled for Meg. He poured himself into her until he was pale and weak and couldn't take it anymore. A Hellion only had so much blood. On the fifth night, he walked to the balcony, opened the doors, and stepped out into the moonlight. He didn't want to leave her alone, but he needed to feed himself. Skeele jumped off the balcony and spread his wings. His glide was uneven, his muscles weak and body drained.

Skeele knew he wasn't supposed to feed off the newly dead souls. They needed a chance to get to a Safe House, to repent. If he upset the balance, the Deacons would want justice. He couldn't wait. He couldn't hunt and he couldn't let the others know that he'd left Meg alone.

He found a house where newcomers were hiding. They didn't expect him. No one expects a Hellion. He crashed through the door and ate them just like the monster Meg had always accused him of being. It was hard to stop and not move on to another house. That's what a shit ton of fresh blood did to a Hellion, made them absolutely feral and uncontrollable. When Skeele's stomach was full, he walked out of the house, went to the sky, and returned to Meg's side. He didn't even leave bones behind.

———

Skeele reminded himself that the last time Meg nearly died, she'd laid in that bed for months while her body healed and her bones mended. Patience was a virtue; it was just that his was wearing thin and he wasn't very virtuous to begin with. He had left Tukka, Chel, and Klaus to train the Hellion new recruits and take care of the last of the fast-dead.

There was a knock on the door. Skeele stood and walked to it. He moved the chair that held the knob, unlocked it, and opened the door.

Noah was there. "Is she still alive?" Noah asked.

"Yes." Skeele cracked the door open further so Noah could see the color that had returned to her cheeks and shallow breaths that had started days ago. Surprised that Noah didn't simply apparate into the room like he typically did. The ghost-man was in a bad way. Ever since witnessing Nightingale's death, Noah hadn't been the same. He never smiled. He stopped with the jokes. It was like he'd died that day as well.

"Has she opened her eyes?" Noah asked.

Skeele shook his head no.

———

Skeele had been sitting in the chair for days, waiting for her to wake. He was tired. Dead tired. After all his blood, she hadn't budged. No muscle tics, no noise from her throat, no twitches from under her closed eyelids. It wasn't looking good. Her breaths were shallow and far between and the wound over her heart was taking a long time to heal. Skeele reminded himself that she'd lost a lot of blood. He was sure the Hellions were cleaning it off the bar for days. And then there was that spell Jed had tried; who knows what that shit had done to her? Skeele cracked his knuckles as he thought about the next step.

The bed was enormous enough. And he was confident she would never know. He moved to the other side and lay down next to her. He sliced his left wrist the long way this time and deeper than ever before. He turned and laid it against her mouth and closed his eyes. If he never woke, at least he tried to save her.

HOLDING OUT FOR A HERO

I dream of Sparrow. My mind is fuzzy and foggy. My limbs feel like they're filled with cement. My eyes are so heavy I can't find the strength to open them. Everything I do is in slow motion. But Sparrow's here, finally. It took long enough. I can smell him, that darkness that led me to him on the Earthen plane. Wood smoke and cigars and burning embers. It seems my realm permeates from him.

Sparrow's wrist is against my mouth. His warm body is finally back in my bed. I've been waiting for this for a long time. I grip his arm, moving from the wrist to bite him along his bicep. He tastes good. Better than pancakes and Twinkies and orange soda.

I push him over onto his back and snuggle close, my lips moving to his neck. He tips his head away, one arm gripping me tight against him. I rub against his hard, muscled body. I want him to bite me. But he won't put his mouth on me, even when I try to move his face with heavy arms that feel like stone. Maybe it's been too long for him. Maybe he's holding back. I don't care. I'll take from him what I want. It's only fair. I lost myself in his memory for so long. It's my turn now. My turn to take what I am owed.

It takes a lot of effort, but I slide my leg over his, my inner thigh resting against his groin. I want to move the rest of my body. I can't find the strength. The blood tastes too good. I can't take my lips off his neck. I moan against his throat. His arm tightens on my waist. Fingertips brush the sensitive skin under my ass. I want to say things to him. I want to tell him I missed him. I want to whisper dirty words in his ear. I want to lick and taste the parts of his body I've been denied all this time. I force my arm to move, tugging, dragging his shirt up. Skin on skin never felt so good.

A deep growl rumbles in his chest.

A thunderstorm drowns out the noise in my room. The sharp crack of thunder. The pelting of rain. I can't make out his words. He's saying something.

"I can't hear you," I whisper in his ear. Biting, tugging, and sucking.

Sparrow's leg moves against mine and I feel the bulge in his pants. I move my hand against his face to turn him. He won't look at me. He must be holding back. Sparrow's always been like that. Chivalrous. Must be the last of his grace. Wait… did his grace come back? I try to open my heavy eyelids, but I can't. They feel so heavy, glued shut. I slide against him, over him. Pushing his clothing away.

––––––––

Skeele

During the night, Meg came alive. She writhed over him; her hips pressing against him, her hands rubbing, her hot mouth feeding greedily. Skeele looked away. She had the worst bloodlust he'd ever seen in his life. Skeele was barely holding on. He gripped the side of the bed frame and squeezed until the wood cracked. He was surprised he had any strength since Meg drained him like a leech.

Whispering in Hellspeak, a language Meg wasn't fluent in, the heavy downpour outside drowned out his words. She'd never know what he'd said. That was probably a good thing.

This was worse than anything he'd imagined. She was hellfire in his arms. Untamed. Wild. Insatiable. She held nothing back, like an animal in heat.

He had to slow her down. Skeele was demon bred, Hellion trained. He could tear her apart if he lost control. He wasn't totally certain she wouldn't do the same to him. She had taken Lucifer's place, but she still looked to be very much human. Small and delicate, even if her smart mouth led one to believe otherwise. She wasn't though, he'd seen her change. And he had entered this room fully aware that he may never exit.

Skeele gripped Meg's hips and rolled the both of them until she was under him. He held her wandering hands against the mattress and ran the tip of his nose along the column of her neck.

"Do it," Meg begged. "I like it. It feels so good." Her hips pushed up against his. "Fuck me while you do it."

Skeele knew she was bare, and he could feel the heat that radiated off her naked body through his clothing.

"Open your eyes," Skeele said, strain in his voice.

Meg shook her head slowly. "I can't. They're too heavy. I'm too tired. Do it, Sparrow. I've waited so long."

Skeele growled and ran his tongue along her neck. "Go back to sleep," he begged.

"I can't," Meg said, pushing her bare breasts against him. "I need you first."

Skeele nipped at her neck. He wouldn't risk taking her blood. He knew that she'd slay him the moment she woke fully and realized what she'd done. The look of shock on her face after the Vermont cabin was forever burned in his brain. Meg felt nothing for him. Wanted nothing from him. Was disgusted by him. That made it easier. At least he'd done his due diligence to protect the throne. That was his fate, his destiny. They bred him for it. He was alive to do nothing more. He fulfilled that promise.

Meg writhed underneath his body. The shirt he'd put on her became tangled and twisted behind her back. She was warm, her stab wounds nearly healed, her skin a bright pink. He moved and looked down between their chests. The stab wound over her heart was still open. At least the bone was healing but he was worried that it was still soft, that his weight could cause more damage. He didn't want to injure her further. Skeele released Meg's hands and moved down her body. It was hard to control himself. If this was going to be the last of his days alive, he wanted to be just as greedy as Meg.

But he couldn't. He knew better. She had to recover so she could set things straight in her realm. No one was going to know what to do with an Angel without hands, and whatever was hiding in that room next door with Jed and Shay. They couldn't be left with an empty throne and the threat of the Seven Kingdoms of Heaven looking for retribution from the Fast-Zombie War.

Skeele didn't flip Meg over and mount her like a wild beast. Instead, he grabbed her hands with one of his, preventing her from finding the horns on his head. He slid further down her body to the vee of her thighs. He would not satisfy his own need, but his mouth would hers.

———

Jed & Shay

Shay paced the room holding baby Thrush. Her arms rocked him quicker than she was comfortable with. Shay thought babies were fragile things that should be handled gently, but Thrush was only calm when he was rocked at a rapid pace. It worried Shay, that she might give him brain damage or that he might develop some strange fondness for being shaken when he got older. Shay tried not to think too deeply about it. The kid had barely survived being eaten during the Fast-Zombie war. Whatever methods she used to soothe him had to be better than what he experienced during that ordeal.

It had been weeks since they left the child in Shay and Jed's care. Every night they still checked his skin from head to toe for bite marks. They'd found none, of course. Only soft baby skin and the occasional diaper rash.

Shay paced near the door, waiting for Jed to return. She tiptoed around the markings on the floor, careful not to disturb the charcoal marks or piles of salt. Jed had protected them all for this long, she wasn't about to put them at risk. It wasn't that long ago that Shay had no idea that Heaven and Hell truly existed. Her prepper parents worshipped other books, like the Farmer's Almanac. Not so much the bible or churches.

Shay and Jed crossed paths in the Midwest. Jed was traveling to California to investigate the zombie horde that was moving like herded cattle. And Shay was simply surviving the apocalypse just like her dad prepared her to do.

Shay paused when she heard shouting from another area of the castle. She had a strong urge to leave the room and find Jed. She looked at the dark-haired baby boy in her arms and remembered her promise. She couldn't leave the room, she could only hope that Jed would come back in one piece.

Shay glanced at the bottles drying near the bathroom sink. Thrush didn't want anything to do with the formula Noah brought. They'd tried everything. Every milk. Cow, goat, sheep, almond and coconut. Thrush didn't want any of it and what he did take, he puked up not long afterward. Shay's clothes were perpetually stained. Jed entered the splash zone, but he usually had towels ready to soak up the baby vomit. Thrush's cheeks were slowly shrinking in size, dark blue circles had started under his eyes. The kid wasn't necessarily sick, but from everything Shay had read, Thrush was borderline malnourished. If this kept on, he'd be completely malnourished quickly.

Noah was anxious about Thrush not eating. He spent most of his time finding something for his son to eat. They'd tried jars of baby food and infant cereals. Thrush would eat it, but it wasn't enough. He needed the milk for a few more months at least.

Shay saw shadows under the door. Someone was outside the bedroom. There was whispering, tapping, and then the door handle turned. Shay moved to the far side of the room, reaching for the spell cast shotgun with runes carved into the metal barrel.

The door opened.

Shay let out a sigh of relief as Jed stepped in and latched the door behind him. He leaned his back against the solid wood door and took a deep breath.

"Is she dead?" Shay asked.

Jed nodded.

"Shit." Thrush stirred in Shay's arms. She rocked the baby again. "What do we do?"

Jed made a face as he skirted the markings on the floor to get closer to Shay.

"She might come back to life. Skeele is going to try something."

"I don't think I want to know."

"It's probably better you don't. These people are freaks."

Shay tipped her head to her shoulder, a motion that told him they might not be so freaky. Shay had seen worse in humanity. Unfortunately.

Thrush started crying. Jed made a bottle of the most recent formula Noah had brought them. He passed it to Shay. Thrush pushed the nipple out of his mouth and gagged on the baby formula. Shay set the bottle down and shifted Thrush in her arms.

Tears started streaming down her face. "This kid is going to starve to death." Shay wiped at her face. "One day we are going to wake up and he's going to be lifeless in his crib."

Shay was crying, Thrush was crying.

Jed stood nearby feeling utterly useless. He couldn't save Meg and he was sucking at keeping this kid alive.

Thrush started nuzzling Shay's chest, leaving wet marks on her shirt.

"There's one thing we haven't tried," Jed said, reaching for his notebook of spells and magic. He flipped the pages.

Shay looked down at the baby and realized what he was talking about. "I don't think so."

"Why not?" Jed asked. "It's natural."

"I'm not his mother."

"You don't need to be his mother. Wet nurses rarely are."

"I've never done this before."

"It can't be that hard." Jed paused on a page and tapped his finger on the paper. "I think I found something that will work."

"Don't you need my consent or something."

"This isn't permanent." Jed paused. "You don't want to try?"

Thrush whimpered in frustration, his little arms and legs were limp.

Shay couldn't watch him fade before their eyes. They'd both promised to look after this baby. "Just do it."

Jed's fingers danced in rhythmic spell casting; he chanted ancient words from his book.

Shay's chest started to feel warm and full. She looked down to see wet marks where her bra was.

"Okay, I think it's done," Jed said as he closed his notebook and knelt near Shay. "Do you want help?"

"Have you done this before?" Shay asked, tears dripping down her cheeks. This felt strange and weird and she wasn't prepared to hand over so much of herself.

"No. But that doesn't mean I'm of no help." Jed brushed his shaggy blonde hair away from his eyes. He set a hand on her knee.

Shay lifted her shirt and pushed her bra aside. She'd never breastfed a baby before, but she'd learned about it in her parent's survival books. There were plenty of chapters on delivering babies and placentas and keeping children alive.

Thrush latched on and ate, and for the first time in weeks he didn't cry or vomit. He simply ate until the tears on his cheeks dried to salt and he fell asleep making faint snoring sounds.

"Was it bad?" Jed asked, moving pillows behind Shay's back so she could get comfortable.

"It wasn't terrible." Shay scooted down in the bed until Thrush was lying flat and she could release him. She looked at Jed. "This is way more than what I signed up for."

"But look at all the fun we're having. I told you there would never be a dull moment with Meg involved." Jed crossed his arms on the bed and leaned forward from his sitting position on the floor. He and Shay were almost nose to nose.

"You should have warned me in Montana that if I followed you, I'd be stepping into some mega shit." Shay pursed her lips.

Jed smiled. "What better have you got to do? Kill zombies and pick dumpsters for food?"

"I didn't get my food from dumpsters. I grew it and hunted for it."

"Okay. But had you stayed, you would have never experienced this shit show. You'd be so bored."

"I wouldn't be lactating to feed an angel ghost baby hybrid." She smoothed Thrush's hair away from his eyes and smiled, relieved that the baby had finally eaten something and kept it down.

"True."

Shay sighed, tired from the long day and the tears. She wanted nothing more than to sleep a few uninterrupted hours, but they needed to talk. "Tell me what happened downstairs."

Jed made a face, but he told her and then they planned, just in case Meg never woke up. What good was life on the run without a plan? Jed and Shay had been running their whole lives, just in different directions until that abandoned gas station in Montana. Jed ran from the Archangels and Demons who wanted to extinguish all Nephilim. Shay ran from a family who taught her to survive, who taught her to never forget, and taught her to never trust. Never trust a man, a woman, family. Because when the sun went down or the doors were closed, the truth would always come out when they thought nobody was watching.

MEG

We go on for days. Feeding. Fucking. Just like animals. Just like creatures of Hell. There's not much thinking, just primitive need. And if I had a rational thought during it all, I'd think I wound up exactly where I belonged.

Between the intimate moments, I have nightmares of dropping out of the sky, nightmares of Hellions coming for me, nightmares of zombies eating babies. But Sparrow wakes me from them. He holds me close and tucks my hair away from my face, whispering sweet nothings into the night. He protects me just like he's always wanted. I have never been more content. This is all I have ever wanted. Me and Sparrow. Sparrow and me. Being invincible together. Even if we never leave the bedroom. If we never have another adventure together, at least I have the memories of all those times we traipsed across each plane trying to figure out who we really were. I could stay forever locked in this bedroom with him. My eyelids are too heavy to lift. That's okay. I know what he looks like; the edges and planes of his body, the touch of his fingertips. I know. I'll never forget because when I'm with Sparrow it feels too good to be true.

———

I stretch, waking to the sound of gentle chirps and a soft whistle. I roll, satin sheets pulling away from my body. I open my eyes and blink a dozen times to focus. Skeele is sitting by the balcony, his back to me. He's feeding the birds like Noah used to do before everything went to shit. I smile at the familiar *tap, tap, tap* of heavy sunflower seeds bouncing on the railing.

It doesn't take me long to realize I'm naked except for an unbuttoned flannel that's falling off my shoulders. I look down and see a bright pink scar over my heart. I pull the sheets up and cover myself. Laying back, I stare at the ceiling and try to remember what happened.

Skeele stands and stretches, his shoulders slump. He looks pale and moves slowly as he closes and locks the balcony doors. He turns to me, face thin and gaunt, and startles. "You're awake," he says as he rubs a hand over his bare head and horns.

I nod, my mouth feeling like it's filled with cotton and sand. I'm so thirsty. My eyes feel dry and heavy like I spent the night in a smoke-filled bar. If I did, this is the worst hangover ever.

"I'll get Noah," he says, walking out of the room.

Noah comes bearing gifts. A Big Gulp sized orange soda, pizza, and BBQ wings. "Sleeping beauty awakens," he says.

I reach for the soda. Noah passes it to me, and I drink greedily.

"What happened?" I ask.

Noah sits. "You don't know?"

I close my eyes and the scenes flash through my mind. "I fed Sparrow a vial of Teari's blood. He changed. He went back to his kingdom." My face pinches. "He stabbed me." My fingers touch the scar on my chest, my stomach, my leg, and arm. I open my eyes. "He tried to kill me." I groan.

Every jab of his dagger flashes before my eyes. I want to scream. I pinch my eyes closed and press my fingertips over the corners of my eyes to stop the tears. I can't cry. I won't cry for him.

Every memory of me and Sparrow dies. Every wish to have him at my side dies. Every song, every feather, every Snowy Owl word... it's all dead to me. Forever. I thought Sparrow was different. We were connected. He was the only one who showed me love and caring and truth. He was my halleluiah, heroin, and reason to breathe. He turned out to be no better than Jim. He is no better than those Hellions from my grandfather's time. No better than the Archangels who locked me up in Babylon and whipped me.

It hurts. Worse than anything. Worse than Jim. Worse than John Lewis. Worse than that day the Hellions came for me on the Earthen plane. My eyes burn. My chest throbs. I want to puke.

Noah watches me, silent. I remind myself that I'm not the only one who has lost someone I love in all of this. It doesn't work. Sorrow is a slippery slope. I can't stop myself from sliding down. It's been so long since I felt like this. Empty. Dead inside. The last time I felt like this we were running from the dead and I didn't know who I was. I stopped in the middle of the road as a horde approached, ready to end it all. It would have been easy back then. There was so much less to think about. Fewer people involved. I rub my face, surprised that there are no tears. I can't do this anymore.

I button my shirt, throw the covers back, and stand;

unsteady on weak legs. I move to the balcony, the walk feeling twice as long as I remember.

"What are you doing, Meg?" Noah asks.

I climb up on the railing, my knees wobbly and arms aching.

"Meg..." there's worry in his voice. But Noah hasn't ever stopped me from doing things. He's the best kind of friend. He lets me make my mistakes and then never lets me forget them.

"Skeele was right," I say. Bird seed crunches under my feet. A sunflower seed peeks out from under the curve of my pinky-toe. It's a long way down. "I need wings. Because I'm going to fly my ass to Heaven and put Sparrow in a fucking grave."

I jump.

Do The Thing You Fear

MEG

I spread my arms, tip forward, and... drop like a sack of shit. The wings don't pop out of my back, there's not even an itch. The familiar scorched grassy lawn gets closer and closer to my face. My flannel shirt billows in the wind.

Noah appears on the lawn, waiting, arms crossed. He looks up at me, unimpressed. I get a sickening feeling deep in my gut. This is going to hurt. Shit. I should *poof* myself somewhere, but as much as I want to live, I want to punish myself for being so stupid. There is nothing better than punishment. Just ask John Lewis. There is nothing better than pain. Just ask everyone. Pain is a lesson in never forgetting. Pain will break every single bone in my body for the second time the moment I hit pay dirt below. If only my wings would break out of my back. If only I could soar like a Snowy Owl on a dark night, the frozen air ruffling my feathers, crystals of snow glistening in the moonlight.

I am not a Snowy Owl. I am not an Angel. I am merely

an embodiment of Lucifer. I make eye contact with Noah. He's smirking. What a jerk. Nothing like a best friend to be smiling before you eat dirt.

Just before I'm about to hit the ground, strong arms wrap around my waist and tug up. Warmth wraps around my back. I'm finally flying but it's by no means of my own. From my periphery I see the bat-like wings of a Hellion.

A familiar voice in my ear. "You could have put some underwear on so the entire castle didn't have to see your bare ass."

He's flying fast. Air rushes into my mouth and I can't talk back. I can barely breathe. I ignore the tears in the corners of my eyes and let the wind blow them away.

Skeele flies away from the burning caves, over treetops and small towns. He finally lands on a single lane road next to a little river dotted with boulders. His heavy boots echo on the steel deck bridge. My bare feet land softly as Skeele sets me down as if I'm made of glass.

Skeele paces away from me. He's tense, his Hellion gear haphazardly hanging on his body. He looks like he's lost a lot of weight since before Sparrow tried to kill me.

"What is wrong with you?" I prod him.

"You were going to kill yourself? After everything you went through?" Skeele is shouting at me. He's lost his cool. It's completely gone. Not that I've ever known a Hellion to have a cool factor, but Skeele is approaching another level right now.

"How dare you assume," I take a step closer. "I was trying to get my wings!" I shout.

"I thought you gave up on that goal?" Skeele shouts back. "Or at least you should have waited until you'd fully healed."

"Don't tell me what to do," I step forward again and point at his chest. "Of all people, you threw me into the sky for the exact same reason. You tossed me so far up into Hellsky I almost puked."

"Yeah, but I gave you time to recover from nearly dying. There was a difference." He tips his head, focusing on a sound in the forest. One hand settles on his blade.

I grab for mine but there's nothing there. Just bare skin. My naked thighs aren't protection against much. Shit.

"Is it a fast one?" I ask, feeling unprepared.

Dark eyes settle on me. "We killed them all. Every one we could find. The portals are still down, and word is that the Earthen plane is rebuilding." He moves his hands to his hips and glares down at me. "It was just a deer or something."

"Fine. Take me home," I order.

"No," his eyes are dark fire.

I close my eyes ready to *poof*, but I go nowhere. Damn. My muscles feel weary, my throat dry. I'm too weak to travel at will. I hate when this happens.

"Take me home," I order, again.

"Not now," he backs away from me. "I'm not done," he says.

"I am the ruler of Hell. Do what I say." I rise up on my toes. It's the only way for me to get taller since I'm barefoot. I really should have thought about dressing for my adventure out the window.

Skeele laughs, sharp teeth gleaming white against his lips. "Don't threaten me," he warns. "Of all situations you're out here nearly naked and without a blade. What are you going to do, bite me?"

"I've done it before," I warn.

Skeele nods and smiles, it's an arrogant move. "I don't think you have it in you right now," he taunts.

I turn and walk away.

"Where ya going?" Skeele asks.

I rub my face and run my fingers through my hair. I look for a street sign or a mailbox to try to figure out where he brought me. I've been down here long enough that I recognize most roads that are close to the burning caves. But I'm not sure where we are right now. I'd remember a steel-deck bridge; there were a few near Gouverneur and they made your ears ring when you drove over them. I walk. I don't know what direction it is, north, south, east, or west but it's in the opposite direction of Skeele. Which is where I need to be headed right now before I do something stupid.

My throat is so dry. I lick my lips and try not to think about the food I left behind in my room. Poor Noah went through the effort to surprise me and I just left it there. I'd kill for a pizza right now. I step on a sharp rock and stumble. Rocks in the road never felt so sharp. But then, I've never gone traipsing around barefoot down here. Jim taught me better. Always be prepared. Always wear sturdy shoes, dry socks, and carry a few supplies in your pack because you never know. Jim's probably rolling over in his grave right now. Good for him. If anyone deserves to roll in their grave, it's him.

There are more skittering sounds in the tree line, leaves crushing and sticks snapping. It's hard to release the memories of the fast-dead running at me, ready to bite. I walk faster, my spine tingling in angst. I try to *poof* again. Nothing. Damn. I should've stayed in bed. I should've snuggled down into the soft mattress and piled blankets on top of me and ate pizza until my heart was content. I should've channeled a pig in mud and stayed put instead of throwing those blankets back and trying to force wings to appear out of my back. There are a lot of things I should've done, but regret is not my strong suit. I'm more of a carry on without compunction type of girl. How does one not regret leaving the house without shoes... or underwear.

I rub my neck; suddenly holding my head up feels challenging. My neck aches. My head fills with fog and I stumble. I step on another sharp rock in the road and go down. My hands hit first, grinding against the loose asphalt and tearing the skin of my palms. I throw my body to the side and land on a hip, trying to save the road-burn to my knees.

"Christ," Skeele's heavy footfalls come closer.

I close my eyes, my eyelids feeling heavy. Suddenly, I could care less about anything other than sleeping for a million years. I rest my head on the pavement and go.

———

There was a time when I would dream of ridiculous things. I'd dream of memories and fears and hopes and I always knew when Nightingale was there, speaking to me through the dreams. You never realize how one person walking through dreams can mess with you, can help you remember that you're not alone, even in sleep. I miss it. She had a way of letting you know she was around, even when she was the farthest away. I've lost those moments though. Because Nightingale died. I watched her die. I watched one of the fast-dead bite a chunk out of her neck and then she bled out. I did nothing to save her. I've replayed it a million times in my head. I cut off Teari's arms, but I couldn't cut off Nightingale's head. Where would that leave us? An Angel without a head or an Angel without a body. Either way, it wouldn't have worked. How would she raise a baby being just a head? I guess her body could have grown back. But then, Teari's arms haven't grown back. So who knows what would have happened if I had chopped off her head. I have guilt from not experimenting with every possible way to save her. We could have sewn her head on another body and turned her into some Frankenstein-Angel-thing. I imagine she wouldn't have been too happy with that outcome. I'd be pissed if I woke up only to find my head sewn on twelve other men's body parts. Yuck.

Without Nightingale, I am left to my imagination as I sleep. I dream of fountains of blood. Chalices overflowing with thick red liquid. Orgies and naked Angels so attractive Michelangelo's David would blush. In my mind I know it's wicked, but it feels so good, it looks so good. There are no babies without mothers, no depressed Angels without hands, no Sparrow stabbing me to death, no Hellions with a mood. I could stay here forever and revel in the indecency of it all. It feels good here. I like it.

But... my legs are cold, and my ass is cold, and my throat is dry even though I've been drinking from the fountain like a horse.

I open my eyes and wait for my vision to clear. The blurriness takes a few moments to pass then I notice the rough-hewn wooden walls and lack of furniture. I'm in a place that looks like the Hellion cabin in Vermont. It doesn't smell like Vermont though. It smells like an old town in winter. Like kerosene heaters and coffee and burning newspapers.

I roll to the side, find a blanket covering one knee, and throw it back over my legs and butt. I snuggle in and try to get comfortable again. But I get that feeling that I am not alone.

Someone is sitting in the room with me. I know that shadow. He's reading a book, using the window for light and the fireplace to warm his feet. I want to lash out at Skeele and tell him to get the fuck out of my space. I know better. Nightingale would have told me to chill the fuck out after terrorizing me in my dreams. And then she would have made me apologize to him. I do what she'd want, in her memory. It's the least I can do.

"I'm sorry," I say. "Okay. I'm sorry." I press my head into the shitty pillow I'm resting on.

"For what?" Skeele's voice is dull.

"I don't know. Whatever I did." I raise my hands then drop them onto the bed in frustration. "I've always done something."

"Usually." Skeele doesn't even put down his book. "There's a vial of blood on the nightstand. It might help."

"Okay." I should thank him. It's just, thanking someone when I don't want to is hard to do. I can't make the words come out of my mouth.

The sound of crisp paper flexing breaks the silence as he turns the page of his book. I can't look away from him, he looks like a freaking Ivy league scholar wearing black-ops gear. It gives me a feeling deep down in my stomach. I know, without a doubt, if something happens to me, Skeele will always be sitting in the room like that when I open my eyes again. No one has ever been there for me like that. No one.

"How long have I been here?" I ask.

Skeele shrugs. "A while."

"Hours?" I ask.

"Two days."

"Jesus Christ." I rub my face, turn, and reach for the vial of blood on the nightstand.

"You drinking that now?" Skeele asks, brows raised in exaggerated questioning.

I hesitate. "I think so."

He slaps his book closed and stands. "Drink it."

I twist the vial and down the thick liquid.

His heavy footsteps cross the room. "I'll be back," Skeele says as he leaves, slamming the door and locking it from the outside.

"Hey!" I shout. "Why did you lock me in here?"

"Because I can't take any more of your shit," he shouts through the door.

He has a point. I cap the vial and set it back on the nightstand before snuggling under the blankets. Warmth spreads from my throat to my gut to between my legs. Yeah, that's why Skeele left. We've been in a Hellion cabin before when the bloodlust was strong. I rub my legs, close my eyes, and imagine doing dirty deeds to someone, someone other than Sparrow, someone big and strong. Someone true and... real.

The next time I wake it's like the wicked thing that I am. My feet hit the floor before my vision clears. There were days when I slept fully clothed, boots and all already on, ready to wake and run. It's been a while. My bare feet stretch against the rough flooring of the cabin. I stand, taking the blanket with me and wrapping it around my waist to cover my legs. I feel disgusting, like I haven't showered in a week. My hair feels greasy, my skin coated in a film of... something.

"You ready to go now?" Skeele asks from the shadows

near the fireplace. He waves his book. "I finished this a while ago. It's getting kind of boring listening to you snore."

"I don't snore," I snap.

Skeele chuckles as he stands. "I won't tell anyone you snore." He crosses the room and opens the door.

Poof.

I go back to my room at the castle. Skeele can find his own way back.

Nobody's Housewife

MEG

I've never been good at cleaning, but I clean my room like a good little housewife. Except, I'm nobody's housewife. So I guess I clean my room like a single lady. Except, I'm not a lady. I find a pile of ripped and bloody clothes in the corner of my room. There's a pile of bloody sheets as well. I make my bed and pick up a pair of shorts from the floor. Hm. I don't remember ever wearing these. I toss them in the laundry. I rearrange the bathroom. I take a shower and get dressed in dark jeans and a wide-neck, black T-shirt. I glance in the mirror and curse the bangs for a moment. My mind wanders back to the scene of the dead falling out of ceiling and killing Nightingale and Jack. My chest feels heavy, my eyes burn. I look away and swallow it down. Tears have never gotten me anything. They won't bring back my friends. They won't fix the fact that Sparrow is dead to me. They won't release Gabriel from his Heavenly cage or fix Teari. I rub my face until the sensation disappears.

After spending some time alone, I remember that I have

a giant mess to deal with down the hall. Most important being the Angel-baby next door.

I leave my room, thankful that there are no moody Hellions waiting in the hallway for me. I knock on Jed's door and wait for him to open.

The door cracks slightly.

"Hey," I say.

"Wow," Jed opens the door further, relief washing over his face. "You're alive."

"Why wouldn't I be?" I ask.

He motions for me to come in. "Last time I saw you, it wasn't looking good." He nods to the bed. "Shay's asleep. It's been a rough night." Jed rubs his face. "The baby is teething."

I glance around the room and find Noah sitting by the crib. He waves one hand at me.

"This last week has been hell, Meg," Jed says, crossing the room to sit. "Thrush wants his mother. He cries a lot. It's heartbreaking."

I maneuver around the runes on the floor, being careful not to disturb the piles of sand and charcoal markings.

"Feeling better?" Noah asks.

I shrug. "I'm not really sure how I'm supposed to feel." I look at the baby in the crib. He looks just like Noah but has Nightingale's eyes. He looks smaller than I remember.

"Speaking of feelings," Jed says. "We can't stay locked up in this room forever. We haven't seen sunlight in weeks. We haven't had fresh air. When are you going to let us out of here?"

"It's not really safe to bring you all somewhere else." I tuck my hands in my pockets. "The Earthen plane is rebuilding. But Thrush can't go there." I shake my head, remembering my childhood. "I won't let him get lost and abused."

Noah's eyes flash to mine. He was there. He knows what I went through.

"Keep them here," Jed says. "Just keep us here, just not in this room forever."

At least Thrush could have his father nearby if he stayed in Hell. The only problem would be making sure none of the Archangels from Heaven come looking for him.

"We need out of this room," Jed urges. It's the strain in his voice that makes me realize his clothes are rumpled and disheveled. Solitude isn't good for them.

"Okay." I pause for a moment to think. "There's plenty of abandoned homes here. We could find you all one."

"They'll need security," Noah warns.

"The runes work well." Jed points to the walls and door that he marked. "No one has come in. Not even a bug. They work well."

"You're going to do an entire house?" Noah asks.

Jed motions, nonchalant. "I've done it before. Do you know how hard it is to hide from Archangels and Demons on the Earthen plane? I've lived this long. I've been doing it since I was a kid. If anyone could rune a house, it's me." He crosses the room to his bag and opens it. "I'm going to need more charcoal, salt, and sand. Depending on the size of the house."

"Okay," I agree. "Okay. Me and Noah will go out later and look for something that's not too far away."

"I'll have to prep it before we all go there," Jed says, zipping his bag.

Noah glances at me and tips his head toward the door. We leave the room and I hear the soft scrapes of Jed fixing the charcoal runes on the threshold after the door closes.

"What about the Deacons?" Noah asks.

I smile. "I've always wanted to kill them. Maybe this is my time."

"Won't you upset some balance if you do that?" Noah asks.

"Nothing is balanced. The Seven Kingdoms of Heaven skew everything for their benefit. I'm not holding back because of the Deacons any longer."

———

Teari's room is dark. Really dark. It's calming. I've found the shadows are comforting these days. Or at least the shadows of my own home are. The shadows of a forest on the Earthen plane or a courthouse in Babylon will still make me want to shit my pants.

"Teari?" I whisper into the room.

"Go away," Teari says. Her voice is dismal, lifeless. Like she couldn't care less about much.

"Where are you?" I ask.

I hear furniture scrape across the floor. "Meg?" Teari asks.

"Yeah."

"There's a table lamp near the door. I can't switch it on since I don't have hands." Teari sounds depressed; there's no life in her voice.

I wave my arms in the darkness until I nearly knock over the lamp, then I steady it and click it on.

"Why are you sitting in the dark?" I ask.

"So I don't have to see what I lost," she replies, voice dull.

I open my mouth to say something, to compare, to let

her know she's not alone. But it seems wrong. Instead, I say, "That sucks."

Her stumped arms crossed over bent knees. "Hi." She's leaning against the wall, her wings slumped and missing feathers. I am reminded of the time Nightingale molted and wonder if that's what Teari's is going through or if she's just depressed like a caged bird.

"What can I do?" I ask.

Teari shakes her head. "I don't know. I don't know anything anymore."

I sit on the edge of her bed. "You know lots."

Teari's quiet. She rocks back and forth as she asks, "Who stabbed you?"

My stomach pinches, my heart skips a beat. "Sparrow," I say.

"Why would he do that?"

I bite my bottom lip to make it stop quivering. There's something about a straight shot question that threatens to rip out your soul. But I'm not going to stew in that feeling. I'm going to embrace the hate for the man I once loved. "I'm sure there's a reason." I stand and make my way to the dresser where there are a few prosthetic limbs. I run my finger over the metallic claws. I never allowed Teari to touch my skin much, but when she did, it definitely didn't feel like this smooth metal.

I turn. She's watching me.

"I don't like them. They feel... unnatural," she says.

"Where'd you find them?"

"Noah brought them." She makes a face.

"He's always trying to fix things." I sigh. "Ever since he died."

"Maybe he's trying for redemption," Teari suggests.

"Isn't it too late for that?"

"Who knows?" She holds up the nubs of her arms and taps them together like Dorothy with her ruby slippers. "Seems I don't know much about how our realms work anymore."

"We'll figure it out," I promise.

"I need you to get me out of this room. I need to do something so I don't go crazy." She pauses and touches her face. "And I can't find Nightingale. She's no longer in my dreams. I think... I think something happened to her." She holds up her arms and I imagine her past mannerisms when she had hands. "She always comes in my dreams. Always. At least once a week to check in. I haven't seen her in so long. Since before I went to find you on the Earthen plane." Her eyes are wide and worried. "I think something has happened to her."

Shit. Something did happen to her.

"You're right," I say. "She's not just missing. She's gone. Forever."

Teari stares at me, her mouth slightly open, her skin pale in disbelief.

"She died when the fast-zombies infiltrated the Seven Kingdoms of Heaven. We went to help. Me and the Hellions. I brought the Basilisk. But... we couldn't save them. Nightingale and Jack died."

"Oh God," Teari's arms settle on the side of her head. "I knew it was bad. Where's Gabriel?"

I tell her about the cage.

"No no no. If Raguel and the others turned on Gabriel, it's not good." She looks at her arms. "If they have him, my home is gone too."

"I'm going to rescue him," I say. "Soon."

"Alone?" She stands and paces. "You can't go alone. They'll eat you for dinner. You need an army. You need to protect yourself." She turns. "Take me." She thumps her arms to her chest. "Take me with you."

"I don't think that's a good idea," I say.

"Perhaps. But it's a distraction." She holds up her nubs. "Maybe if I go back, I can get my powers again. Maybe I could heal. Maybe..."

All I can think is that I cannot lose another friend. It's been too many too fast. Teari is one of the few from the Seven Kingdoms of Heaven that I can tolerate. If I lose her and something happens to Gabriel, I'm alone in this mess. Completely alone. My stomach pinches. I can't do this alone. I can't go back to feeling like I did before I found Sparrow and found out who I was. Teari can't fight with me.

"You're not going to risk your life for me." I motion to her arms. "Wait until you're healed before jumping back into this mess feet first."

Teari moves toward the door. "Fine, but I'm going to need you to take me somewhere besides this room."

It seems to be a repeating theme. Everyone wants out of their room. No one gave a crap all the times I was locked up. Truthfully, though, Jed and Shay didn't have anything to do with those times. Teari was an accomplice once. I wonder if she regrets doing it to me. I don't like the idea of locking up my friends. They deserve freedom, but I'd also like them to stay alive.

———

"If you're going to go up against a healed Sparrow, you are going to need a little more training," Chel suggests from the shadows of the Hellion lair.

Between my hands, I slide my glass across polished wood and watch the reflection of thick blood sloshing. "I didn't train to go up against Lucifer," I say.

"Lucifer didn't know you," Chel says. "He didn't spend time with you and study your ways."

"You're going to need to surprise him," Tukka says. He crosses his arms and leans on the bar. "You're going head-to-head with a warrior who has trained his entire life."

Klaus moves to the wall of weapons, thick fingers tapping on swords and blades and guns. He chooses a small dagger and turns to me. "Sparrow nearly ended you with a blade smaller than his hand. Imagine the damage he would do from the sky."

"If he picked you up and dropped you," Skeele interrupts.

"I know." I stop him with a raised palm. "I know what happens in that scenario."

"So let us train you," Klaus suggests. He slides the small dagger across the lacquered bar.

I stop the small weapon with the slap of the palm and twirl it by the point before wrapping my fingers around the grip and lifting it. It's a very different feel than my blade and I wonder how it would feel to jab with this tiny thing. Must feel good since Sparrow used something similar on me. The thought of him makes my stomach twist. My scars ache in remembrance; it happened so fast, so quick. Like a dancer to a rapid beat of drums. *Stab, stab, stab. Poof.* My chest twinges. I look down at the scarred tattoo. I should've known better.

"Yeah," I agree suddenly. "You can train me."

———

Tukka waits in the center of the dirt patch outside the entrance to the burning caves. The sun has set and Hellsky turns chilled, the moon providing dim light. Tukka's boots crunch on the ochre dirt. I glance at the others, watching from near the front of the cave entrance before turning to face Tukka.

He's tall, muscular, his skin scarred from years of battle experience. Tukka's eyes meet mine. He's determined to teach me something tonight, I can see it. I've seen that glint in a man's eye before. The glint in the eye of a Hellion. I'll never forget it. We circle each other, sizing each other up. Without my blade, I'm feeling really inadequate as I grip the small dagger Klaus gave me. There's something about a blade that only cuts in the grip of its owner.

Without warning, Tukka lunges forward, his dagger flashing in the dim moonlight. I barely have time to move, holding my dagger up, it rings out as hilt clashes against hilt. Tukka moves back one step before lunging again, this time he jabs lower. I jump to the side, grind my elbow into his tipped shoulder, and shove him away. He sweeps his arm as he falls to the side, grabbing my ankle and trying to drag me down with him. I hop on my free foot as he rolls onto his back. He loses his grip on my ankle, and I step on his wrist before slamming my other foot down on his chest. Tukka is fast, but bulky. He's playing nice, keeping his wings out of the way. He could've used them by now.

I step away from him. "You're being too easy on me," I say, annoyed. "You're better than this."

Tukka smiles, showing sharp teeth. "I saw you the night

you killed your grandfather, you're better than this too."
He moves to his feet fast. He slaps the dagger out of my
hand.

"Nice," I mock after he laughs.

He jabs. I dodge and weave around his jabbing arm, on
the third one, I punch his wrist and kick his opposite thigh.
He drops the dagger. I kick it away. Adrenaline is pumping,
my heart races as I focus on showing Tukka I'm not as weak
a fighter as they think I am. Danger has lurked around every
corner of my life. I may not have wings, but I'm scrappy. I
can punch a throat or kick some balls as good as the rest of
the white trash girls I grew up with. Been doing it for a
while now.

Tukka swings his big body around and his shoulder
lands in my gut, sending me flying backward a few feet
before I land on my ass. Dirt grinds into the palms of my
hands as I try to catch myself.

"You fuck," I groan. One of the daggers is under me, the
handle pressing into my spine. I grab for it then roll to free
my hand. What luck.

Tukka comes at me again. I thrust my right hand out
and cut him in the thigh with the dagger. It slices through
his leather pants and thick skin like they are nothing more
than soft butter.

"Ah," he kicks my hand.

But it's too late. Fresh blood does a good job at getting
me off my ass. I scramble to my feet and show my own sharp
teeth. Shit. The adrenaline from fighting and fresh dripping
blood...

Tukka's eyes go wide before he launches himself into
the sky with a powerful jump, his leathery wings beating
hard, sending dust and sand airborne.

I jump and grab at his boot. Gripping on, I dig my nails

into the thick leather and grab for the laces with my free hand.

He shakes me off like I'm nothing more than a snake in the leaves.

I drop to the ground like a cat and laugh. "Are you afraid now?" I ask.

Fresh blood drips down his boot to the ground in front of me. Tukka hovers a few feet over my head. "I've seen that look before. You don't fight fair."

"What look is that?" I ask.

"The same look on your face before you drained Lucifer dry for all of Hell to see." He beats his wings, rising higher, farther from me.

"No one in the Seven Kingdoms of Heaven is going to fight fair. Not even Sparrow." I tamper down the desire to drain him of every last drop of blood in his body. I don't need Tukka dead. I need him at my side.

"I think we're done here," he says as he flies toward the caves.

Noah moves closer. "That's my Meg, always making friends." He claps me hard on the back.

"What can I say?" I spread my arms. "It's a gift."

Noah laughs lightly. "Shitty gift."

"Better than nothing." I make my way to the entrance of the caves and tag this instructional moment as a win for Meg.

HOUSE HUNTING

MEG

Teari and I trudge through the streets of Centralia. We walked from the burning caves, past the smoking vents in the hillsides, and headed west on Big Mine Run Road. Centralia in my realm looks very similar to the abandoned town in the Earthen plane. There's uneven, cracked roads and a few chipped white painted houses with moss covering rotting wood. I'd say, it's probably the only place that closely resembles itself on each plane. But that's what an abandoned town with fire burning underground will get you. It's a two mile walk to the crossroads of Centre Street and Locust Ave. There aren't many houses here; most are torn down, and the lots filled with forest trees. There are crumbling structures with rotting clapboard and thick mossy covered roofs further down the road. Those won't do for Thrush.

"Which way?" Teari asks, her wings making scraping sounds as they drag on the pavement, turning gray with dirt and leaving bits of white feathers behind.

I didn't intend to leave a trail of crumbs so we can find our way home. A small white feather rolls under my boot.

"There's Saint Ignatius Cemetery down Locust Ave." I point. "Or Centralia Fire company No. 1 in the opposite direction."

"Not optimal for a baby," Teari says. "There aren't any houses?"

We walk a little further.

"No houses that I'd want my family living in," I say. "I'm afraid the roof would cave in on most. At least the chapel in the cemetery is stone and solid, same with the fire company building."

I pull my jacket tighter around myself to ward off the chill of the evening air. We've been searching for a house for baby Thrush for days. We started farther away, in bigger towns with nicer houses but agreed that distance was not our friend. The Hellions and I need to be closer.

Teari rubs her face with the sides of her arms. "I can't believe we still haven't found a house for them."

Rain falls, and Teari wipes the drops from her cheeks. "Let's look at the cemetery."

I nod in agreement.

"He can't be here for long," Teari points at the ochre dust under her feet. "Maybe we shouldn't even be wasting our time looking for a house."

"He's safer here," I argue.

"No, you don't understand." Teari presses her lips together and sighs. "I didn't know how to tell you. He'll turn into a Nightjar if he stays here."

I don't enjoy looking stupid, but I've got no choice right now. I don't know what that is. "Explain," I say.

"Nightjars are manifestations of the souls of unbaptized children doomed to wander the night sky," Teari clarifies.

"He is a child of the Seven Kingdoms of Heaven. Nightingale would not want that for her son. He must go back. We must baptize him in the fountains of Babylon."

"I'm not sure that's a good idea," I say. "There's no one to take care of him up there."

"He has an uncle," Teari presses, her voice low.

"Let him grow up with a murderer? No." I shake my head and wrap my jacket tighter.

Our footsteps echo on the deserted streets. Every so often, a dimly lit streetlight flickers when we walk under it.

"He'll protect Thrush," Teari says, trying to adjust her cloak.

I do my best not to look at her skeptically. "Protect him? Thrush needs protecting from him, not by him. I can't hand over a baby to the man who stabbed me to death."

Teari takes a deep breath, hesitating. "He could change. We all change throughout these immortal lives."

"No one changes," I snap back.

"No?" Teari challenges. "You haven't changed?"

I shake my head, my eyes downcast. "I haven't changed much. Taking the throne in Hell hasn't prevented me from doing wrong and making mistakes. It hasn't prevented me from being selfish."

Teari touches my shoulder; it's strange, not the light touch of fingers but heavier. For one of the few times in my life I don't pull away. "All right, Meg. You haven't changed. You're still the rash, foul-mouthed woman-child I met last year who couldn't tell the difference between Demons and Angels." She smirks.

"Still can't tell the difference," I mutter.

"Also, you've changed," she says. "For the record. You shouldn't downplay how far you've come."

I nod, wanting to change the subject. I don't enjoy

talking about myself like this, it has always been easier with some self-deprecating humor instead.

The chapel in the cemetery comes into view.

"It's not that bad," Teari says as we walk toward the front door. Tall, brown grass sweeps at our shins as we make our way across the cracked sidewalk.

"The windows are high," I point. "The door solid."

Teari nods. "It's not a castle but it could do."

I push my shoulder against the heavy door and shove it open. Dust motes swirl in the evening sun rays shining through the window. My daddy always said I'd burn to a cinder if I stepped foot inside a church. It's never happened and he wasn't my daddy. But the fear always hits me as I step foot across the threshold of any religious building. Not here though. This feels like stepping into my castle.

Stone floors, arched windows, and an open space make up most of the chapel. The walls are lined with dusty shelves dripping with old wax and burnt-out candles. As we explore, I find there are living quarters off to the side with a small kitchen.

"It could be quiet," Teari says, knocking on the stone wall with her elbow. "No one outside would hear much through this."

"That's good." I kick at some sticks and leaves that made their way in. The place needs to be cleaned.

"Will the dead stay out?" Teari asks.

"It would be hard for them to get in here." We walk to the back of the chapel. "There's only two doors to reinforce."

"And the roof?" Teari looks up.

"It looked like slate when we were walking up. I'll have the Hellions check it out. We could make it strong so nothing can fall through."

Silence passes for a few moments. It would be a tragedy for Thrush to die the same way his parents did. I'll do anything to make sure it never happens.

Rain patters on the rooftop as it begins to downpour outside.

"I don't see any leaks," I say, inspecting the ceiling. "That's promising."

Teari shivers. "It's cold enough to freeze the balls off a pool table." She looks out a nearby window. "Does it always get this cold when the sun goes down?"

I shake my head. "Only in winter."

"Lucky us," Teari mutters. "What about a fence around the exterior so they could go outside in the day?"

I nod. "The Hellions could build it quickly. We can scavenge for panels."

Teari tucks her arms into jacket pockets. "This could work. It could be a home." She clears her throat. "It doesn't fix the Nightjar problem."

"Ask Noah," I say, trying to hide the frustration in my voice. "Thrush is his son. But, what I know is that Noah will not want that baby a realm away from him. Not after losing Nightingale. None of us wants him out of our sight. Sending him back to Heaven is going to be non-negotiable. I know Noah will agree."

Teari frowns and walks in a circle, thinking. "Just for the baptism at least?"

"I don't think that's a good idea."

"Save his soul."

"I already did!" I shout. "He almost died once." Memories of the moment the dead fell through Nightingale's roof flood me. I press my hands against the sides of my head. The biting, the blood... "If you had been there–"

"I wasn't," Teari shouts back. "Because I was in a

hospital in bum-fuck Pennsylvania. Remember? You left me on the Earthen plane, alone, half-dead." She holds out her arms. "I would have loved to be there to fight, but I couldn't be."

"You're alive now." I say, trying not to take her words personal.

"Am I?" She steps closer to me. "Am I alive? Because every day I feel like shit. I feel like I shouldn't be here. Like I cheated death or something."

"You want me to get you a shrink?" I blink. "Life sucks ninety percent of the time for all of us. Just because I have my hands, doesn't mean I haven't lost *other* things." My fingers itch to pull the blade off my thigh holster, but I know she's not coming at me like this to threaten me, she's just working through the spaghetti in her mind. "You healed me before. I didn't hold it against you. I did what I had to do to keep you alive. You would have done the same for me."

Tears slide down her face and Teari comes at me with arms open. She hugs me, burying her face into my neck and crying, heaving as large sobs wrack her lithe body. I'm not a fan of hugs, I'm more of a tap them with a broom and tell them there, there type of gal.

I guess we all have to mature some time. I hug her back, careful not to touch her wings and knock off any more feathers.

"I just feel so useless," Teari says though the sobs.

"I have met a few useless Angels. That's not you." I pat her back, awkwardly.

"You don't have to say that."

"I wouldn't if I didn't mean it."

———

We leave the chapel when the rain stops.

"Everything looks different at night here," Teari says.

"Sure does," I agree.

Moaning from the forest makes my spine straighten. The memories of the fast zombies are hard to bury. I grip the blade at my thigh.

"Shh," I say, holding a finger to my lips. "I hear something."

"Wing beats," Teari says.

I look up and see one of the Hellions pass overhead.

"They're protective of you," Teari says quietly.

"Yeah," I walk toward the caves. "Let us walk," I say into the night. "Just for once give me a moment of peace."

The wing-beats soften and grow more distant, their whispers replaced with the chirping of crickets and croaking of toads in the thicket.

"There was a time when you hated them," Teari reminds me. "When you couldn't be near them."

"That time still lingers. It's a process I've been going through." I try not to think about the gaunt, pale Skeele I woke up to just a few days ago and how I almost cared about the unhealthy way he looked for about five minutes. "I wouldn't dwell on my feelings for them."

Teari moves closer to me, hearing the rustling in the forest. "They'd do anything for you," she says. "That's a good thing."

Last time I gave a shit about someone doing anything for me, it got me in a lot of trouble. It doesn't mean much anymore.

Loyalty is a cage that's only as strong as those surrounding you.

Rescue Me

Gabriel has been trapped in the cage for weeks. His once magnificent wings looked torn and tattered, either from him trying to escape or something they did to him. We are quiet on our approach, so quiet Gabriel doesn't turn until just before we reach him.

Gabriel smiles wide, "Lord knows my Meg would come save me." He grips the bars of the cage. "Get me the hell out of here." His eyes are tired, his face pale.

"That's what we're here for," I say.

"I know why you're here," Gabriel said, nodding to the shadowed Hellions behind me. "Why are they here?"

"Because I need help," I say. "And they do what I tell them."

"Fair enough," he says with a sigh.

Skeele and Tukka pry at the bars, testing them. Next comes the big guns. Skeele starts the angle grinder. The noise is loud. We stand back, waiting. Sparks fly like fireflies.

Gabriel looks toward the building in the distance. "Get

me out or they'll be coming soon. For the love of Pete, let's get this show on the road."

"Can you go faster?" I urge Skeele.

He glares at me. "Going as fast as I can."

I focus on Gabriel. "Who put you here?"

"That asswipe Raguel." Gabriel palms a fist and cracks his knuckles. "As if cleaning up the mess from those zombies wasn't enough to deal with. I'm going to end him."

Metal clangs as one bar falls away.

"There's something you should know, Meg," Gabriel grips the bars opposite the sparks. "Sparrow's back."

"I know," I interrupt.

"He's not what we remember." Gabriel's forehead wrinkles in concern. "He's very different. There's something wrong with him."

"Maybe this is his true self," I reply.

"There's more..." he trails off. "You know with his family curse his head has never been quite right."

Metal clangs again as more of the bars to the cage fall away. The racket will bring a Legion soon.

"I don't care." I say. "I'm going to kill him. It's a non-issue. His curse might as well be my revenge."

Gabriel nods, knowingly. I'm sure he's heard what Sparrow did to me. Being my father and all, I'm surprised Gabriel didn't end Sparrow himself. But then, why deny me the glory of revenge? My father knows me well. I'm out for blood and if anyone knows this version of Meg, I'll drain whoever does me wrong.

Skeele turns off the grinder, tucks it in his bag, and shoves the cut bars. Gabriel steps out. Free. That was too easy. I scan the empty sidewalks of Babylon. Not a soul in sight. Either they don't care I'm taking Gabriel or there's some shifty shit going on.

"We don't have any portals in Hell," I remind Gabriel. "There's only one way in."

We grab hands.

Poof.

Noah appears with inkpots and a handful of sterile needles. He drops them in front of Jed.

"Let's go," I say to Jed. "Get your tattoo gun."

Jed turns to Shay, "I'll be right back."

"It's going to be a few hours," Noah warns. "At least. I'll stay with him."

Jed looks uneasy. Shay looks uneasy. They haven't left this room in days, and they've been taking their new job of babysitting very seriously.

"It's fine," I say. "We just need some ink."

Jed crosses the room to grab his tools and breathes something quietly to Shay. Then he follows us out of the room.

I lead him to the second floor. There's an empty room near the stairwell with chairs and a table and good lighting. I open the door and wait for Jed to enter.

It only takes him a minute to see Gabriel waiting in the corner.

"Oh no," Jed backpedals. "Nope. Nope. Nope."

I grab his arm. Noah slams the door.

Gabriel squints at Jed. "Well, I'll be damned," he murmurs.

"I have spent my life avoiding Archangels and you brought me to one." Jed looks ready to lose it. His eyes are wide with fear and anger. "Is this some sick joke?" He glares at me. "I knew I could never trust you, Meg. Never. The things I've done for you and now this?"

"Calm down, boy," Gabriel bellows. "I'm not here for you." He frowns. "Damned surprised to see you upright and down in this realm," he raises his palms, "but the more days I live, the less this shit surprises me."

"He needs the runes," I say, holding out my arm. "He needs freedom from the other Archangels."

Jed tosses his equipment on the table. He glares at me. "This is not what I signed up for."

"We're in the same club," I move closer to Jed. "Gabriel is my father. The other Archangel's are rallying against him. Including Sparrow."

"Fucking Angels," Jed mutters, shaking his head. He points a finger at me. "You owe me big time for this." He sets his equipment on the table and starts prepping to tattoo Gabriel. "You owe me for the rest of your life."

"Done," I hold out my hand, pinky extended. "Pinky promise. I am forever in your debt."

Jed jerks his hand forward, curling his pinky around mine and staring into my eyes. "I am a forbidden creature. They will always hunt me."

I nod, understanding. Jed and I aren't all that different, he just doesn't realize it.

Jed picks up one inkpot that Noah brought. He sets it aside and motions for Gabriel to lay his left arm out on the table. "We'll do both," he says. "If you can handle it." Jed smirks.

Gabriel rests his arm on the table and Jed gets to work.

"Would this prevent Sparrow from finding Thrush?" Noah asks, tipping his head toward Jed, watching.

"The runes?" I ask.

Noah nods.

"I'd assume." I say. "But, wait. Are you suggesting tattooing a baby?"

Noah presses his lips together and tips his head in a maybe expression.

"I don't think that's a good idea," I say. Something just seems very wrong about tattooing a baby. I've done a lot of awful shit in my life, but I draw the line at that.

Happy Little Trees

Teari is helping me paint the chapel in the cemetery. Actually, she's spending most of her time pointing out what a shitty painter I am.

"There's a big spot by this window," she points with the nub of her left arm. On the right she's wearing the prosthesis with a claw for a hand.

"Why don't you paint it?" I ask, wiping a dot of paint off my face with my sleeve. The sage green color stains my black shirt.

"I can't," Teari replies, moving farther down the wall with her inspection. "There's another here."

The door blasts open and I drop the paintbrush. Skeele walks through with Gabriel, carrying a couch.

"Jesus Christ," I mutter, picking up the brush and searching for a rag.

"That's going to stain," Teari says flatly.

"Well maybe you should help clean it up," I snap.

"Where do you want this?" Skeele shouts. There's an edge to his voice, beyond simple annoyance.

"Wherever," I shout back. I find a rag on the nearby table and use it to mop up the paint splatter.

"I guess, you could always cover it with a rug," Teari suggests with a disappointed sigh.

"Is this good?" Skeele asks as he drops his side of the couch.

Gabriel follows suit and drops his side as well. A large thud echoes throughout the empty room.

"What the heck?" I startle with the loud noise. "Are you trying to wake the dead?"

"Thought they were already awake down here?" Gabriel chuckles.

The moment between me and Skeele is tense. "Just try not to damage the furniture. This isn't a pigsty Hellion lair. A baby has to live here," I remind him.

Skeele stomps out of the room.

"What the heck is going on with you two?" Teari asks.

Gabriel sticks around for the drama.

I wave, dismissing her concern. "Something crawled up his ass and died." I find the paint and go back to painting the wall.

Gabriel chuckles at my comment. "Never a dull moment in this realm. Absolute chaos. Better than when I did my time down here as a Hellion. That was eons ago though. I like what you've done with the place, Meg." Gabriel slaps me on the back as he walks through the room causing me to drop the paintbrush again. A large plop of sage green stains the floor.

"Fucking-a." I grab the brush. I didn't think about Gabriel remembering his time as a Hellion. Sparrow's mind was so screwed up I just assumed that my father wouldn't remember either.

Skeele kicks the door open again, this time he's carrying a coffee table. "Where do you want this?"

"Up your ass," I reply.

Teari laughs.

Gabriel's eyes widen.

Skeele drops the coffee table and leaves.

"Hey, try not to ruin every piece of furniture you bring in here," I shout.

The door slams. I slap more paint on the wall and swipe the brush furiously. My stomach growls. I try to ignore it.

"Maybe you should eat, Meg," Teari warns. "You're getting hangry."

"Who will paint?" I ask. It's nice to be needed for a menial task and not something life or death or end-of-the-world-esque. Painting is easy. Painting doesn't involve zombies or Hellions or murderous Angels or hunting for slimy Basilisk. I could paint all day with these low standards.

"I'll paint," Gabriel offers. He holds out a large hand and I notice the healing runes twisting up his forearms.

"Don't get your robes dirty," I motion to the paint splatter all over my clothes.

"Ditched those for good," Gabriel smiles. He's wearing jeans and a green flannel shirt with the sleeves rolled up. If it weren't for his giant size, he'd look absolutely normal. "Give me the brush. You go... get something to eat."

I hold the brush between two fingers and let Gabriel take it. "Are you staying here?" I ask Teari.

"I think that's safest right now," she says, inspecting my subpar paintjob.

"Fine." I wipe my hands on my pants and walk away. As

I get close, the door flies open and I catch it with my hand before it hits me in the face.

Skeele's standing there, a nightstand in his hands, oozing bitterness. He doesn't apologize; instead he walks through the threshold and around me. His movement brings a breeze that smells like smoke and pine. It's a comforting smell, makes me feel like I am home, makes me hate him even more.

I slam the door closed as I leave. I jog down the steps and the walkway before veering off the path and walking between the headstones. Some are half-sunk into the ground, some are covered in moss and lichen.

Living in a graveyard is kinda odd but it's not a dangerous place to raise a child. There's nature and calm and hopefully we can keep Thrush hidden long enough that he'll have a peaceful childhood. Every child deserves that.

I sit on a broken headstone and stare off into the distance. Sooner or later, I'm going to have to have a conversation with Skeele about his crappy attitude lately. I can't have my first in command being a douche. He still listens. There's just, something else going on with him that needs to be cleared up.

My stomach growls again. Damn. I had pancakes and eggs and sausage for breakfast. It must be a different hunger. The one I try to ignore.

Noah shows up. Always when I need him most.

"I brought you this," he passes me a bowl. "It's cherry pie."

"Of all things," I say just before digging in.

"I was hoping the red color would help." He sits next to me. "You know, because you need to eat blood and you haven't had any in a very long time."

The pie is sweet, the crust flaky; it even has real whipped

cream on top. I chew and swallow before replying to him. "I'm fine. I've survived plenty of dry spells."

"I worry about those around you."

I look at his face. Noah stares off into the distance, his expression placid, not letting on to what he really means.

"I won't harm anyone," I say as I take another bite.

"You say that, but I've seen you turn in the heat of the moment." He clasps his hands together. "I want you to stay away from Thrush until you've had blood." His voice is low, like he doesn't want anyone else to hear.

"I wouldn't hurt him," I say, trying not to let Noah's distrust ruin my day.

"There's plenty you'd promise me, Meg. But the truth is," he turns to look into my eyes. "I can only do so much to keep my son safe in this realm, and while I will be forever grateful that you brought him here, I will always worry that he'll be present during a moment that you can't control yourself."

Anger boils through my veins. Being hungry for blood makes it worse. "Everything I've done..." I take another bite of the pie to prevent myself from saying something truly terrible to him.

Noah wraps his arm around my shoulders. Usually, I'd pull away or push him away, but something's going on deep inside my soul. Something Noah can sense; he's always been good at that kind of stuff. He's always been there to get me into trouble, there to get me out of trouble, there to bring me back to reality.

"You've done a lot to help us, Meg. We'll never forget it." He squeezes me tighter. "This blood thing is new, and I've seen you at your worst. Thrush can't be around you when you're like this."

"You don't want me to see him?" I stab at the pie and

shove more into my mouth. I try to focus on the deliciousness of the flaky crust.

"Not unless you're full. On the real stuff. Not the cold stuff the Hellions live on. Fresh blood, Meg. That's the only thing that keeps you reasonable."

Perfect. Here's Noah giving me an ultimatum that I'll never be able to fulfill. Damn him. I don't have Sparrow to feed from and the next time I see him it will be to kill him, so there goes that. And randomly feeding off a stranger will turn me into a hoe because I know how I get when the bloodlust is at full tilt.

"I know you'll figure out something," Noah says confidently.

I'll figure it out. Sure. This is one of those moments when I should cry silently as I stuff my face and let my best friend console me. I blink back the tears.

"Choke it down, Meg," Noah whispers, knowingly. "It's okay."

A bluejay lands on the gravestone next to us. I try to whistle a light trill, but pie crust gets stuck between my front teeth and it looks like I'm spitting my food out.

"I got you," Noah says just before whistling to the jay.

It talks back with a jabber of chirps and whistles and song and I am transported back in time, months ago when we were sitting in my room feeding the birds on the balcony. Me and Noah and Nightingale and Sparrow. I have to stop dwelling on the past, but the hard thing is, that past was the best months I've ever had in my pathetic life. It's hard to let go and move beyond that. Memories of joy aren't so easy to bury. I want to set them on a mantle in my mind and reminisce on Sundays and Christmas mornings. But two of those people are gone now. Dead and dead to me.

Jed and Shay are walking down the road. Jed's carrying

Thrush. They bundled the baby in a hat and snowsuit. Shay is carrying a heavy backpack and if I know her it's packed with everything she needs to survive for a week, at least. They walk toward the chapel. Jed notices me in the cemetery.

I wave but stay put because Noah's grip on my shoulder tightens. A warning. The realization comes to me that this will forever be my view of Thrush's life. He's the closest thing I have to remember Nightingale. It seems everything must be kept at arm's reach, or further. It's probably better that way.

I finish eating the pie. I cram it into my mouth to fill the ever-growing void of darkness in the pit of my chest. It's hungry, starving, never fulfilled.

"You should go home, Meg. It's getting late," Noah suggests.

I stand to walk away, the tall grass swiping at my knees. Something hits hard under my boot. I bend to pick it up.

Seems I've found Sparrow's book. *Birds of Paradise* rests in my hand, caked in dirt and stained from the rain. "I've been looking for you for ages," I say.

"Haven't seen one of those in a while," Noah says.

"I lost this one when the Scarecrow came."

"Guess it's time to return it to the library." He holds out his hand, ready to do my dirty work as always.

"No," I say. "This isn't from the library. This is from someone's house. And I'm going to bring it back to them."

Noah's lips tip in a playful smile as I test the weight of the book in my hand.

———

"Has Thrush been baptized yet?" Gabriel asks as we sit down to dinner.

I'm grumpy because only half the people I want to see are here, and... I'd prefer sucking my dinner out of someone's jugular. Thoughts like that are beginning to feel normal, shameless. I nearly take the solid mahogany table draped with food for granted. Candlelight reflects off the polished wood, illuminating the wood smoke haze on the ceiling. Small bodies writhe up there. Basilisk babies have left their tank and taken to the ceilings. They follow me from room to room like puppies. It's creepy.

Teari drops her fork. I try not to stare as she fumbles with the prosthetic arms. At least she's trying to use them. That's an improvement.

"No baptizing that I know of," I say, scooping a giant spoonful of mashed potatoes onto my plate.

Gabriel grumbles something about the fountains of Babylon.

"What?" I ask as I pour gravy. A lot of gravy. I pour until I think it might fill the void in my gut.

"He must be baptized," Gabriel says as he cuts into a roast and serves himself a heaping slab.

"He's going to be a Nightjar, it doesn't matter," Teari says from her side of the table. She's holding a spoon between the claws of her right arm prosthesis.

"Why are you so certain he will turn into a Nightjar?" I ask. "Have you seen this happen before?"

Gabriel and Teari look at each other.

"What?" I urge.

"It's more than lore," Gabriel says. "You could ask the archangel Raphael. It happened to one of his children."

"How?" I ask.

"The story goes he had a child with a creature other than an angel," Teari says, concentrating on the spoon handle. "Her name was Demore. She was born of darkness. Which can only mean she was born in this realm. Which can only mean Raphael–"

"Was getting his freak on," I interrupt.

Gabriel chokes on his wine.

"You haven't heard Demore's call?" Teari asks. "All that time you spent wandering down here?"

I tip my shoulder up and make a face. "I heard a lot of shit."

"It's like plip-plop," Teari says. "It's like the sound of someone's eyes being pulled out."

"I don't think I've heard that," I say.

"Thrush should be baptized," Gabriel says. "If not, he'll be satanic. A creature of Hell."

"You'll never escape him because you'll hear him calling at night. Plip-plop. Plip-plop," Teari says, her tongue clucking the p's.

"He might even pull out our eyes," Gabriel says.

"You'll never forget that sound." Teari continues, "Plip-plop."

"I heard it once." Gabriel says. "Will never forget it."

I focus on Gabriel. "You heard it once?"

He nods, silently.

Must've been during his time as a Hellion.

"Plip-plop. Plip–" Teari says in a sing-song voice.

"Shut up," I warn her.

Teari stops, eyes wide as she grips the spoon with her claw and scoops a tomato into her mouth. She bites, red juice and seeds coating her lips.

"Is it a curse that can be broken?" I ask.

"By baptism," Teari says, around her mouthful of food. "I told you."

I shake my head.

"Who's getting a baptism?" Noah appears. He sits opposite me at the table and swipes at the blonde hair near his eyes.

"Meg," Teari says.

"Nope on a rope," I say, stabbing a giant piece of roast and cramming it into my mouth so I don't say something stupid.

Gabriel pushes his chair back and seems to be completely disinterested in the conversation suddenly.

"Have you ever heard of a thing called Demore?" I ask Noah.

Noah narrows his eyes and glances at everyone.

"Plip-plop," Teari whispers.

"Have you heard it?" I ask. "When you're out there searching for all the shit I ask for?"

"I hear a lot of things," Noah says.

"But have you heard the plip-plop of eyeballs being plucked out by a Nightjar?" I ask.

Noah leans back in his chair. "That's very specific." He shakes his head. "I can't say I have."

"It's a scam," I say, looking at Teari and Gabriel.

"Scam?" Noah asks, propping his feet up on the table and crossing his legs.

"Not a scam," Teari says.

I stare at Gabriel. He can't lie to me. "All lore has truth. He should be baptized. Just in case."

"Are you talking about Thrush?" Noah asks, dropping his feet and leaning forward in sudden interest.

"Thrush will be a Nightjar," Teari says. "Unless he's baptized in the fountains of Babylon."

Noah looks at me. "Nightjar?" he asks.

"These two are telling me that without being baptized, Thrush will turn in to a creature of Hell and his soul will be doomed to wander the night sky," I say.

"Plip-plop," Teari says.

"Meg's a creature of Hell, she's not so bad," Noah says, staring at Gabriel. His smile goes flat.

"Meg is half-darkness," Gabriel says. "She's where she belongs. Your boy on the other hand–"

"Is half Astral, half Angel," Noah says.

"From the wrong side of the Earthen realm," Gabriel says with a frown.

He would know. Gabriel and Noah both fell for a girl from the wrong side of the tracks. Nothing is easy after that. Especially with children involved. The jar of feathers on my nightstand tell a similar story.

"The Astral is darkness. It's nothingness." Noah runs his fingers through his hair and rubs his neck. "Thrush is half-darkness."

Gabriel circles a finger in the air. "Not this darkness. Hell is a different place."

"So I take him to the Astral," Noah says.

"There's nothing there," I say.

"I will be there," Noah argues.

"You can't raise him in nothingness," I say. "Don't subject him to a lifetime of loneliness. He's alive, he can't live in dreams and outer-space."

Noah taps a finger on the table, thinking. He knows it's not right. He can't deny Thrush a childhood of poor decisions and teenage high-speed chases. If he didn't live through all of the typical childhood mistakes and traditions, he'll be... nothing.

"Baptizing him is easy," Gabriel offers. "It can't hurt to just do it and prevent the Nightjar business."

I swallow the food in my mouth to say, "So we take him to Heaven and Gabriel will baptize him in the fountains of Babylon. Then we come back here. Good to go. No issues."

"It doesn't sound like a no issues kind of thing," Noah says. "You've never gone to Babylon without a complete shit-show ensuing."

I nod. "True. But maybe I go beforehand and kill Sparrow. Then there's not much to worry about." I talk around the food in my mouth. "When we rescued Gabriel no shit-show ensued."

Gabriel chuckles.

"What?" I ask.

"The other five Archangels will come for you," Teari warns. "Anyone with a brain knows that."

"Maybe I kill them too," I suggest.

"You can't go killing everyone in the Seven Kingdoms of Heaven," Gabriel says. "You have to maintain some balance."

Tukka breaks into the room, hurried, only pausing when his eyes meet mine. "There's a Deacon here," he says. "And it wants to talk to you."

"Fuck that." I cross my legs and get comfortable in my chair.

Noah, Teari, and Gabriel continue talking and planning.

"He says he's not leaving. He has a message from Sparrow," Tukka says.

The room goes silent.

My mouth wants to spew some vulgar shit. Rage fills my chest. I could slay the room with the rage. I stand, knocking my chair over and gripping my hands into fists. "I don't want to hear his name. Ever."

I leave the room and follow Tukka. He takes me to the cave entrance, and I am grateful that he didn't let the scum Deacon into our home.

"Sparrow sent a message," the Deacon says. One finger tugging at the collar of his black button-up shirt.

I stare.

"Sparrow's message is..." The Deacon looks like he saw a ghost.

I flash sharp teeth. "Spill it. My dinner's getting cold."

The Deacon clears his throat. "Sparrow says he wants his nephew back. Now."

"I don't know anything about his nephew," I lie. "As far as I'm concerned, his nephew died in the Fast-Zombie War alongside his mother and father."

"We know he didn't," the Deacon argues.

"How do you know?" I take a step forward.

The Deacon takes a step back. "He knows the boy is in this realm. We know he's here."

"Then go find him." I say, taking another step closer, ready to run him off my property like a hillbilly with a rifle and a copy of the Constitution in his back pocket.

The Deacon backs up.

"I have a question before you go," I stop the Deacon.

He pauses.

"Where is Demore?" I ask.

The Deacon's spine goes straight. "Don't say that name."

"Why?"

The Deacon turns and runs away.

———

"Are you going to take this stuff in to them?" I ask Teari, motioning to her one arm with the prosthesis.

"I guess I could. You don't want to go?" she asks.

I remember Noah's warning. I can't see Thrush unless I've been drinking fresh blood. And I haven't been drinking fresh blood. All I can see is Teari's jugular beating and hear the blood rushing through her veins. It's been distracting me the entire walk here. I'd be lying if I said I didn't think about draining her dry and leaving her body under a pile of brush near the firehouse. Hunger makes me think things I normally wouldn't.

"Take this stuff." I help get the bag over her shoulder. It's filled with salt, holy water, charcoal pencils, and weapons. Noah has been bringing over five-pound bags of rock salt but I've been collecting the finer stuff from the castle kitchen. "I can't go in there. He has it warded against me."

There are runes etched over the doorframe, more burned into the thick, wooden door. Salt lines the sidewalk. These past few weeks the Hellions built a ten-foot fence around the cemetery. There are more symbols burned into the fence and I'm pretty sure if I touched the latch holding the door it would burn my hand.

I hear the lighthearted giggles of a child on the other side. A few bubbles float into the sky and over the fence.

"He's happy," Teari says with a smile. "That's all we can ask for." She opens the gate and leaves me standing alone on the other side.

I walk the fence and check the runes and markings that Jed made to protect him and Shay and Thrush from being found or hurt. I inspect the Hellions' work and kick the fence in a few places, testing it.

"Stop it!" A shout comes from the other side. Jed's voice.

"I was just making sure it's stable," I shout back.

Hushed wingbeats hover nearby. The Hellions are watching. They're always watching. It's like they're uneasy. Like they know I could snap in a heartbeat. They're not wrong. I can feel it.

I keep walking, thinking about all the scary movies I watched as a kid. Dead cats coming back to life and corpses digging their way out. I recall the night Pet Sematary played on the TV when I was six to help me fall asleep. I never slept that night. I shiver at the memory.

Up ahead, there's an indentation in the tall grass. I walk closer, slowly, praying it's not a petrified cat. Green grass is a stark contrast to the black clothes the body on the ground is wearing. I'd recognize that getup anywhere. The crumpled form of a Deacon lies not ten feet from the fence.

Meddling bastards. I wave to the shadow in the sky to land. I shove the body with my booted foot and roll it. Stiff limbs fall back with a thud.

"Oh gross." I cover my mouth.

The Deacon is missing his eyeballs.

Plip-plop. Teari's sing song voice fills my head as Chel lands next to me.

"That's unfortunate," Chel says as he surveys the nearby forests. "Haven't found a dead Deacon in a long time. Actually, I've never found one."

"I wish I could exterminate every one of them," I say, looking up. More Hellions are on their way.

One of the new recruits lands opposite Chel. "Go back, get Gabriel," I instruct. He takes off as others land.

"What happened to its eyes?" Chel asks.

"A Nightjar or meddling Angel," I say.

"The portals are all destroyed. How would an Angel get here?" Skeele asks as he lands.

"I'm sure they'd find a way." I search the grass around the body, looking for clues.

The grass around the body twitches. "What was that?" I ask, moving closer. The Deacon's body convulses. Arms and legs jerking slowly then becoming violent. We all take a step back as the corpse moves, reanimating to something very un-Deacon-like.

Skeele readies his blade.

"Wait." I hold him back. "See what it does. I want to know what we are dealing with."

The Deacon twitches to its feet, its head jerking from side to side. Without eyes it can't see, but it can hear.

"What in the name of Christ...?" Gabriel asks as he lands next to me, his white Angel wings mostly healed from his prison stint in Babylon.

That's all the dead Deacon needs. A hint of noise draws movement. The Deacon runs toward sound; mouth open, jaws snapping, throat hissing. He doesn't move slow like the dead who typically walk my plane. No, he moves fast. Fast like the walking dead of the Fast-Zombie War.

Gabriel is quick with his blade. Skeele lets him go in for the kill. Gabriel slices the head off the Deacon and the corpse drops to the ground.

"That was interesting," I say, a million questions circling in my brain.

———

"I thought the fast ones were all dead?" I ask the group of Hellions.

"They were," one replies. "There are no portals to let any in."

"It must've died here," Gabriel says. "Died here and turned here."

"They were fast before because they drank Angel blood," I say. "That Deacon drank angel blood?"

"Perhaps not willingly," Skeele says.

"I don't think he drank the Angel blood willingly," Chel says, pointing to a scab on the Deacon's wrist. It could be from a needle.

The Hellions collect the body. Skeele takes the head, gripping it by its hair. Chel and a new recruit grab the body under the shoulders and drag it away. I don't want them flying with body parts. I don't want Jed or Shay to see what just happened outside the walls of their safe zone. They are risking their lives to watch over Thrush.

They drag the body away, down the street and across the way as we search the cemetery for clues but find none.

There's a thin line of smoke as they burn the body.

I meet with the Hellions to discuss the plan to keep Thrush and Jed and Shay safe. We settle on a team of Hellions, the best of the newbies doing around the clock patrols.

"Next on the agenda is Sparrow. I'll be going back to the Seven Kingdoms of Heaven to kill him," I say.

Skeele grunts from beside me. He mutters in Hellspeak after everything I say. Until I can't take it anymore.

"Why are you so goddamn moody? I ask.

Hellfire burns in his dark irises. The energy in the room shifts.

"I'm not moody," he makes a sound deep in his chest like a growl.

"Whatever," I mutter, annoyed.

"Everyone out," Skeele says loudly, pointing to the door.

The Hellions leave. I barely hear the door latch. I'm staring at the bagged blood in their fridge behind the bar, thinking of lowering my standards. I've drank it before. I'm not sure what's wrong with me now, why it's so hard to maintain control.

There's a sound behind me. I turn to a pissed-off Skeele. "All you care about is fucking Sparrow. You are obsessed. Let me tell you a little story, Meg. You want to know why you're upright and full of energy right now?" He stares.

"Noah gave me–"

"It has nothing to do with Noah. It has everything to do with the fact that we were locked in your bedroom for a week straight. You nearly drained all my blood coming back to life." His hands flex into fists at his sides.

"Okay. Well, thanks for that," I snap back.

He steps closer, invading my personal space. I can feel heat radiating off him. I tip my chin up.

"It wasn't even that." One hand falls on the wall behind my head as he leans closer, the tip of his nose touching my earlobe.

"It was all the fucking we did that you don't seem to remember. That's what's been pissing me off the most. You nearly killed me."

Just the Tip

MEG

The tip of my blade touches his chin. "That did not happen. I would never."

"Uh huh," he mocks. "That's a nice little birthmark you have on your upper thigh."

My breath catches. "That's not a secret," I say.

"Do it. I like it. It feels so good." His hips press against mine as he backs me against the wall. "Fuck me while you do it." He grips my chin. A hot tongue licks the side of my neck.

Now that sounds exactly like something I'd say. I dreamed I was with Sparrow. I guess all we did wasn't a dream. I look up at Skeele's face. Every memory, every recollection I have of that time; I erase Sparrow's face and paste Skeele's in there. Fuck.

It wasn't that bad. The things we did... It actually felt really good. So good. Too good. Seems the bloodlust screws with my reality. In my defense, I was nearly dead. I wasn't in my right mind. We all make mistakes. But, the more I think on it, was it a mistake? Seems Sparrow was the biggest mistake of my life. Skeele... maybe not so much. Sparrow tried to kill me, but Skeele never has.

His gaze doesn't break mine. His hand feels hot on my skin. I shiver as the mark from his tongue dries on my neck.

"I don't nearly kill anyone when I take their blood. I end them. I drain them dry," I say.

"Well, you left a few drops of life in me," Skeele says.

"Why would I do that?"

A sinful smile creases his lips. "You must enjoy having me around."

He could be right. I could enjoy having him around. He's decent enough and makes good decisions. He's scraped my battered body off the ground more than once and watched over me as I've healed. He could have been much worse. He could have been like the Hellions of the olden days. But he's not like Vine and the others. And I know deep down I do like having him around. He respects my lead, he offers help, he keeps the other Hellions in check. I couldn't ask for a better first command. He's also never tried to kill me. He feeds me when I'm hangry. What more could a girl ask for?

Skeele tips his chin up and presses his hard body against mine. Yes, I like it.

"Watch it," I warn.

"What are you going to do? Bite me? Jump off a balcony half naked? Obsess over the one man who tried to kill you?" His eyes are fire. "Make me move furniture?" he snarls.

"Well, you did a true shit job moving the furniture. Pretty sure you cracked most of those tables. I won't be asking you to do that again," I say.

"Good."

He tips his head to the side, ever so slightly. And I can hear the *whoosh-whoosh-whoosh* of blood rushing through his jugular.

"You haven't had fresh blood in weeks," Skeele says. "Everyone can tell. You're moody and bitchy and everyone is afraid of getting bit."

"You're a bastard." If I nearly killed him before, I might kill him now. "I'm not a rabid dog."

"Do it, Meg," he says. "Use me. You've been doing it for a long time. All the way back to the cabin in Vermont. Why stop? Now that you know the truth, you're free to decide. Eat." He leans closer, the tip of his nose rubbing against my ear. "If you want to fuck, I'm good with that too. It's been weeks since you writhed over my body. I won't hold back this time like I did all the others."

I close my eyes and try to tamper down the thirst. Now that the offer is on the table, my throat feels drier, the ache between my thighs harder to ignore. I could shove him away, or... I could use him, just like he wants me to. He is my Hellion Commander, the closest thing I have to a partner in this mess. It can be no strings attached. I learned my lesson with Sparrow. Just feed and fuck. That's all. Fill the need because I can't go head-to-head against Sparrow with that bottled blood the Hellions eat.

I smooth my hand over his chest, over his shoulder and rest my palm on his neck. "Don't get too attached," I say, leaning closer, licking his jugular.

One hand slams into the wall behind my head, the other curls around my waist pressing us closer together.

"Never," Skeele says. "Already forgot all those other times happened. If you didn't rule this place, I'd have already forgotten your name."

The bastard.

Poof.
I take him to my room.

Payback's a Bitch

Poof.

I return to Sparrow's Kingdom. Strong, filled to the brim with fresh blood. I stand in the shadows at the edge of the forest. His house has been demolished. The basilisk bones are gone. There is a new house built further back, this one less grand than Remiel's home. It looks more like the cabin Sparrow lived in while he was nothing more than a Legion Commander in Gabriel's Kingdom. As I observe, I wonder if he has rooms in the basement where he likes to lock up family members just like Remiel did.

I grip *Birds of Paradise* by the spine, the book is heavier than I remember. That's good because I have big plans for this book.

Poof.

I'm at his door.

Poof.

I check the back door.

Poof.

I look through the windows.

Poof.

I'm standing at the foot of his bed. He's sleeping. A tall, blonde Angel-woman sleeps next to him. I can hear her blood pulsing through her veins. The *hush-hush-hush* of slumber. It's so soft. Relaxing. Slow. A lullaby.

How times have changed.

Sparrow once told me, "*I am your monster, your saving grace, your everything.*" He asked, "*Will you love me forever?*" He promised, "*...we'll be invincible together.*"

It was all lies. Lies darker than a cold winter night in Gouverneur. Darker than a Demon's son filling my head with deceits and my belly with child. Darker than what those Hellions did when they stormed my house. I thought I'd seen darkness before but seeing Sparrow like this and rubbing my fingers on the scar over my heart tells me otherwise. I've lived through his dark lies, but I am darkness now. I sit on a throne of bones. I rule a kingdom of the dead. I may not have wings, but I will have revenge.

Sparrow rolls. One eye peeks open. Ireland grass green. I will never forget. Before he can sit up straight, I throw *Birds of Paradise* at his head with all my might.

Sparrow blocks the book from hitting him in the face with the quick movement of his hand. The heavy book falls on the blonde, the corner of the spine hitting her ear. She wakes up and starts running her mouth.

"Who is that?" she shouts. "Sparrow?"

I could tear out her throat.

Poof.

I throw back the covers and grab her by the hair at the nape of her neck.

Poof.

I take her to the grassy knoll between the house and tree-line. She's screaming. Whoever this chick is, she's not composed or strong like the other Angels I've met. She slaps at me; weak, untrained, pitiful.

"What are you doing?" she screams at me and cries like a child.

I shove her away and she falls.

Sparrow comes running out of his house. No shirt, black wings, low slung loose pants. Damn, if I didn't want to kill him...

The blonde scrambles to her feet, screaming.

Poof.

I lift her by the arm. Her blood is really pumping. I can't ignore it. Not with him watching. The desire to hurt him as much as he's hurt me is strong.

"Don't do it, Devil," Sparrow yells, pointing at me.

I do it.

I grip her neck and tilt her head to the side, then I sink my teeth in. Just a little taste to see what's so special about her. There's no tingle of ancient blood, nothing that lights my veins aflame like royalty or special powers. It's worse; the fact that Sparrow chose her, nothing extraordinary. He prefers soft weakness and someone so pathetic. I suppose she's pure, untouched, probably even stupid like a barbie doll. Maybe that's what turns him on now.

She faints and drops to the ground as I let her fall, her heartbeat slow and steady. She'll live to tell the story of the morning Meg came for Sparrow.

Sparrow disappears for a moment. He can still poof to travel it seems. He returns a second later, his blade ready and glowing. I reach for the blade at my hip and take a few steps to the side, readying myself. He could go after the girl or come for me. It's only a moment before he comes running toward me.

Poof.

I move behind him.

He turns, blade raised. I hold my blade up and they clang together at the hilt. He's strong, pushing against the hilt of my blade. I drop to the ground and roll away, swiping at his ankles.

Poof.

He's straddling above me. I punch him in the knee.

Poof.

I move away and get to my feet.

Poof.

Sparrow is behind me.

Poof.

I travel faster and faster, appearing behind him, at his sides, low to the ground. I kick him in the shin, the thigh, the balls. Then I move further away.

Sparrow pauses. It seems his ability to poof is weak. I remember those days, when the ability was new and I needed to be full health for it to work. But he could only travel because he drank my blood. The power will be gone soon and he'll have to travel by foot or motor.

Poof.

I slice his thigh.

Poof.

I slice his arm and slam my blade against the arch of his wing. Black feathers fall.

Poof.

I watch him from a few hundred yards away. Sparrow runs toward me, the wounds on his leg and arm dripping. I lick my lips, do my best to ignore it. Even after feeding from Skeele and the dumb girl, I want more.

Poof.

I move behind him.

Sparrow must've anticipated that. He's turned, his blade moving, he hits me in the upper arm, slicing deep.

Poof. I move away.

He points at me. "How'd you like that, demon bitch?"

His words are hurtful. Even though I hate him, each new example of how he's changed hurts. I recall the stab wounds, the pain. I use it. Nothing is stronger than pain.

Poof.

I grab him by the hair and climb his back like a hyena.

He grabs my injured arm, squeezes hard and pulls me off him, throwing me to the ground. I land on my back, the breath slammed out of me.

"No, you don't," Sparrow says through gritted teeth. His heavy boot lands on my neck, the tip of his blade pressing into the soft skin beneath my chin. "This is where I end your reign." He leans down, his wide shoulders casting a shadow over me. "Grace for grace."

"I never had any," I say with a smile.

"There are rules. One realm cannot obliterate another realm's policing force." Sparrow reminds me. "I'm the last one. You can't kill me."

"You're full of shit," I say, watching the blood drip down his arm.

"Those dead things killed them all," Sparrow says. "And you sent them."

"I didn't send anything. They licked your blood off that wall. Yours and Teari's."

His face doesn't flinch when he says, "You're lying."

"Nope."

"Raguel said–"

"He's wrong," I reply.

"But you..." Sparrow says. "I remember all those lies you

confessed to me." His eyes narrow. "Lying lips are an abomination to God."

"I've been told he doesn't exist. What does it matter? The Angels lie more than anyone I have met. More than me. You're not supposed to be able to lie but it's all you asswipes do up here." I open my mouth as a drop of blood falls from his arm toward me. Yum.

Poof.

I move from under his foot to a good hundred feet away. I point my blade. His blood tastes good, strong. He's definitely leveled up. I guess that's what taking the crown does. He is the Raven King with his blackened wings.

"I want my nephew," Sparrow says.

I shake my head. "Died with his parents," I say.

Sparrow's eyes narrow. "There was no body." He grabs his blade, readying for another round. "He'll turn into something else. He won't stay a boy for long."

"I have no reason to care."

"Demore will come for him."

I embrace my inner liar and dig in deep. "I don't know what you're talking about."

Sparrow smiles. "Has she already come for him? We're missing a Deacon."

"Could care less about a Deacon. They should all die if you ask me."

"They maintain the balance of the realms."

"Bullshit," I say. "They meddle and toy and disrupt."

"So you know about the dead Deacon?" Sparrow asks with another smile, catching me.

I've told so many lies I can't keep them straight. Maybe the truth will set me free. Maybe I should just spit the truth like bullets at his head.

"You let these bastards lock up my father," I say. "You let

him sit and rot in a Babylon cell." I tip my chin. "There was a time when you would die for him. For me. What about that?"

"Gabriel lied for you. He forbid the others from holding you accountable for the Fast-Zombie War."

"Unpossible," I use Sparrow's word against him. I guess it's not a lie if they're just spreading ignorance. They don't know the truth so they fabricated their own.

Sparrow makes a sound. "Your snake killed everyone."

"Believe whatever bullshit you want." I ready my blade and bend my knees, prepared to fight. "I came here to kill you."

Sparrow sprints, running for me, blade raised. Black wings spreading, he launches himself into the air.

Shit.

A second pair of white wings appear in the sky. Raguel. More flying angels appear behind him. Five to be exact. The surviving Archangels have come to help their brethren. Word must've gotten out. I turn and find the blonde is gone. She must've run for help and run her stupid mouth.

I don't want to leave, but I don't want to die here. I point at Sparrow with the tip of my blade. A threat if I ever gave one.

Poof.

I go home. Disappointed. My only satisfaction was throwing that book at Sparrow's head and watching it hit the blonde.

———

"Where were you?" Tukka asks as I appear in the hallway outside the Hellion lair. "You look out of breath." He sniffs the surrounding air. "Have you been fighting?"

"Mind your business," I warn.

The door to the Hellion lair opens quickly and Gabriel is standing there. "You're bleeding." His eyes zero in on the cut on my upper arm, concern wrinkling his brow.

"It's just a cut. I need–" I start to say.

Suddenly Skeele comes stomping down the hallway. "Come here," Skeele calls.

I stand my ground.

Gabriel tips his head, intrigued, taking in the dirt on my skin and sweat, the blade with drops of blood secured to my thigh.

"Don't be so nosey," I warn him.

"I only have concern for my daughter, who has clearly been up to something."

I raise my chin. "You forget, this is my realm. I do what I want."

Gabriel steps back and spreads his hands with a little bow. "I yield." He looks into my eyes. "Be careful."

Poof.

I go to my room. I clean my blade and set it aside. Then I go to the bathroom to get a good look at the slice in my arm. It aches. Blood is oozing out. I pinch the skin surrounding the cut and see white bone. Saliva fills my mouth. I might vomit. I can deal with a lot but looking at my skeleton is a little much.

I get my shirt off and search the cabinets for bandages. Teari's healing powers used to be really convenient. She could have fixed this cut in a few minutes. I find some gauze and antiseptic under the sink. I stand, my gaze falling on the tattoo of the sparrow. I want to scratch it off. I should've known better. I broke the first rule of getting tattoos: never put your boyfriend on your skin. It always ends badly.

There's a loud slamming sound as my bedroom door opens and thuds against the wall. I step out of the bathroom and find Skeele standing in the doorway.

"Can I help you?" I ask.

He enters my room and slams the door closed.

Shit. I'm in trouble.

"Did you go there alone?" Skeele asks, stepping toward me. His eyes roam over my body before focusing on the cut.

"I don't have to tell you where I go or what I do."

"Right." He sniffs the air. "But you smell like him. You smell like the putrid air of Heaven. You let him touch you?" Skeele's fuming.

"Calm down," I warn.

He stands one foot from me, the muscles in his shoulder and neck flexing. His hands make fists. "I am calm."

"I didn't let him touch me. I went to kill him," I say.

"Is he dead?"

"No."

"Why did you go alone?" Skeele asks.

"I wanted to kill him on my terms."

Skeele walks around me and turns on the shower. "And how did that work out?"

I look at myself in the mirror. Blood drips off my elbow onto the white countertop. I look pale, tired. "Not so good."

Skeele is behind me, inspecting the cut.

"It's to the bone," I say.

"I am nearly tired of seeing your bones," he grumbles.

"Of everyone I've ever met, ever killed, ever come across, I've never seen their skeleton like I've seen yours."

"It's that bad, huh?" I joke, my laugh cut short by a quick intake of breath from the sharp pain in my arm.

His fingers touch the tattoo of a spattering of stars across my left shoulder and move to the anchor on my ribcage. "I like this one the best." He pushes the waist of my jeans down, revealing the heart on my right hip. He licks the cut on my arm and it seals the wound, staunching the bleeding.

"I warned you not to get too attached," I say.

He makes a face that's hard to read. "Telling you what I like doesn't mean I'm attached." He unbuttons my jeans and shucks them down my legs in swift, rough movement.

Jesus. That was hot.

He stands and leads me to the shower with his large, warm hand on the small of my back. "Wash, rinse, repeat." Skeele orders.

I want to tell him I give the orders around here and that I don't take orders from him. But I'm trying to be better to those who help me. I keep my mouth shut and step into the shower.

I wash, thankful that water isn't seeping into the cut on my arm. Soap would've burned like a bitch. Skeele waits near the door of the bathroom. He's leaning on the counter, one arm crossed over his chest and the other holding a book.

I wash my hair and wonder where this guy keeps getting books and newspapers. He's the only person I've ever seen read in this castle.

When I'm done, I wrap myself in a towel and open the shower door. "What are you reading?" I ask Skeele.

He flashes the cover at me. Different Seasons it says in red.

"Where did it come from?" I ask.

"The library." He makes a duh face.

"You just always seem to have a book when I'm injured." I point out.

"It's because I have to prepare for the long haul of sitting around and watching you come back to life. I stash a book. Or just keep one in my pocket. Because listening to you snore is boring." He pats the large cargo pocket of his Hellion gear.

I dry my short hair and brush my teeth. While I'm scrubbing away, the cut on my arm breaks open. "Ah," I say as it aches worse than before.

Skeele sets his book down and moves closer. He grabs a clean towel from the drawer and presses it to my arm. "Guess we better fix this."

My stomach clenches. He just fed me less than twenty-four hours ago.

"Don't be embarrassed, Meg," Skeele says. "I know it's nothing." He picks me up and takes me to the bed.

———

"Y ou still want food?" Noah looks around me to the mound sleeping on the bed. "It smells like sex and blood in here."

"Don't be a hater," I warn. "I was injured." I point to the bandage on my arm.

"Looks like you're still injured," Noah says. "Ok. Fine. I take pity on you. What do you want to eat?"

"Two large coffees, with four creams and four sugars. Three Jelly donuts. And an enormous pile of crispy bacon." My stomach grumbles at the thought of a sweet and salty breakfast.

"You're a pig," Noah mocks with a smile hinting at the corner of his mouth. "But I will get this food for you. Because it is my duty to serve."

"Maybe, drop some donuts off with Jed and Shay and Thrush too," I suggest.

"Babies can't eat donuts." Noah frowns. He's so serious, so unlike my old Noah, but I guess we are all different these days.

"Live a little. Maybe the others would like surprise breakfast," I say.

Noah disappears.

I press at the gauze wrapped around my arm. There's a little blood seeping through which is strange. I would have expected it to heal after having fresh blood. It was a deep cut. Maybe it just needs more time.

Skeele moves, still asleep. The blankets are barely covering his ass. The deep vee of his spine and firm back are on display. Memories of last night fill my mind. There was lots of biting and positions I haven't tried before. My cheeks flush as I remember my favorite.

Noah appears. Coffees and plates of food. "Get that look off your trash face." He sets the food on the table. "I saw the way you were ogling at that poor Hellion boy."

I laugh. "He's not a boy."

"Hm." Noah looks at Skeele. "Definitely not. Does this mean you're broken heart is fixed?"

My spine stiffens.

"I guess it was too soon for that question," Noah says, looking out the window. "Poor sucker doesn't know what he signed up for."

"It's nothing serious. Just a living buffet of food. Remember. That's what you demanded I do. So that's what I'm doing."

"And having a little fun too." Noah's voice is dull. "I gotta go. Enjoy the coffees."

Skeele groans. He rolls to the side and shoves a hand out over the mattress. His face pinches. "No," he growls. His eyes are closed.

I stand and walk closer.

His body tenses and twists. Sweat beads his head. He groans and mumbles.

"Hey," I say.

He doesn't hear me. He's having a nightmare or something. I crawl across the bed and set my hand on his shoulder. He's hot, warmer than ever. I shake him. "Wake up."

Skeele's eyes open suddenly. He glances around the room before his eyes land on mine.

"I think you were having a bad dream," I say.

He reaches up, one hand sliding up the side of my neck and around to the nape, gripping the hair at the base of my skull. He pulls me closer until our lips are almost touching. "You should eat," he says.

"I just ate last night and Noah brought coffee and donuts."

He sniffs. "I thought I smelled that. I thought it was you smelling like breakfast." His lips move across my jaw to my neck. "Just have a quick snack before that sugar-laden crap you eat," he asks. He moves my legs with his free hand and rolls me onto my back.

His tongue licks my neck, my collarbone. He slides the shoulder strap of my tank away and takes my breast into his mouth. It feels so good I close my eyes and let him explore. My hands rub his shoulders, his neck, the back of his head before gripping his horns.

He mutters in Hellspeak.

"What did you say?" I ask.

He pauses his sucking. "Touch the horns, prepare to ride." He chuckles as he tugs on my shorts, removing them in pieces. Next goes the tank. "No one touches my horns," he says.

I let go. "Oh. Sorry. I didn't realize." I bite my lip to stifle a moan as his tongue explores the vee between my thighs. He tugs me lower on the bed, until we are face to face again.

"I didn't say to let go," he says placing my hands on his horns again. "Don't go to Babylon alone ever again." He says. "Promise me." He moves my legs apart with his knee. He grabs a small knife from the nightstand and cuts his wrist, holding it over my lips.

"That's not fair." I want the blood more than anything. More than his warm body. More than his sinful tongue and erection.

"Promise me." He presses the drips of blood to my lips and then pulls away. "Promise."

"Ok. Fine." I lick my lips and close my eyes. My throat feels hot. My lower abdomen throbs with want and need. "I won't go alone."

He presses his wrist to my lips and lets me feed. "Don't go alone again. Take someone, anyone. Just don't go alone."

These Hellions have become far too concerned. I file it under things that annoy me, close my eyes, and focus on control.

The blood is good. His thickness and length that fills me, even better.

———

SKEELE

Skeele watched her sleep. Propped up on his elbow, his other hand hovering over the bandaged wound on her upper arm. There was something wrong with it. She'd healed faster from worse and the blood soaking the bandage caused concern. He touched her dark hair, the line of contrast as it fell on her pale skin. Hell had never seen a woman on the throne like this. Never someone so small and soft and without wings. Skeele knew she could turn into a monster. He'd seen it the day she killed her grandfather, he'd seen the spark in her eyes when Tukka attempted to train her to sword fight, he'd seen it wavering on edge with her shifty moods. That didn't stop the others from talking. It didn't stop the Hellions from being extra cautious. They were afraid of her weakness, but he knew she could slay every one of them in a heartbeat. She'd barely stepped into her strength. That worried him. She teetered on the edge of true power.

He glanced at the bite marks on his arm. Demons are always hungry. Fresh blood made it harder to control. Skeele had to watch himself before *his* darkness was out of control, he didn't want to return to the old days. Meg deserved better. He'd vowed to be better.

Skeele wanted nothing more than a few more hours sleep; they'd been up most of the night and Meg had taken a little too much blood. But he couldn't close his eyes. The dreams had started the day Sparrow chose him to be Hellion First Command. They worsened the day he watched Meg drain Lucifer of life. It was always the same. Some type of fighting, her being injured, him praying that she'd wake up. Except, she never did in his dreams. She shriveled to a corpse and turned to dust. And it was always in Babylon. If Skeele did anything in his life it would be to keep her out of that city.

Skeele shook his head. He couldn't close his eyes. He had to watch her, just as he'd done all this time. It was his duty. He scanned her back, the swell of her hips. The rest—the blood, the sex—it was a benefit of the job. Or at least, that's what he told himself. He remembered her warning: don't get attached. He reminded himself that she felt nothing and was most certainly disgusted by him.

Skeele rolled out of the bed, found his clothes and his book. He grabbed a coffee and donut from the table near the balcony.

Poof. He went to his quarters and avoided the walk of shame. It was bad enough Meg didn't want him. He could handle the teasing from the Hellions, but the cold shoulder from her hurt. Even if he was simply doing his job. He had to be careful though, traveling on a whim was something new he'd never experienced, and he knew it was from drinking Meg's blood. It wouldn't last, so he enjoyed the power while he could.

———

MEG

Gabriel and Clea are standing on the lower landing of the winding stairwell. They don't hear my footsteps, and I slow, crouching near the banister to watch them. Suddenly I am transported back in time, the forbidden child who never had a home with her parents, watching them from the shadows. I close my eyes and imagine what it could have been like if my mother had lived and the two of them stayed together. We could have been a real family. I could have turned out much differently having not been raised by John Lewis. My throat feels thick as I imagine dinners at a large table with a boisterous Gabriel and serene Clea. Maybe they would have had more children, maybe the fractured bloodline wouldn't have ended with me.

Gabriel and Clea whisper in the shadows. Gabriel leans his shoulder on the wall, smiling, looking like a teenage boy. Clea looks up into his eyes. He says something and she laughs. Gabriel leans closer to her, touches her hair, pausing when his fingertips go right through the strands. Nothing will make you remember that your only love is a ghost like permeability.

I stand and keep walking down the stairs. My footsteps become louder and Gabriel finally notices me. He clears his throat and steps away from Clea, their intimate conversation changing into a formal hello and goodbye. Gabriel passes me on the stairs with a nod.

I stop next to Clea.

"Child," Clea says, concern marring her face. "What are you planning?"

"Things," I say. "I'm planning things." I don't tell her the truth for fear she'll talk me out of it.

"Whatever you do," Clea says, "This is not a lone wolf battle. You need the others. They need you."

"It's just easier to do it myself. Never could count on another soul before, why start now?"

"Times are different, child. You are different. You took the throne. Enjoy all the accoutrements." Her cool fingers touch my cheek. "I think I was wrong." Clea says with a frown.

"About what?"

"I handpicked Sparrow. I saw it in the stars that he would protect you. I told everyone." She looks out the window and over the treetops, her gaze lost in the clouds of Hellsky. "I was wrong. Whoever I saw, it wasn't him." Her image fades until she disappears completely.

I stand on the landing of the stairs alone. A pinching sensation intensifies in my gut. *It wasn't him.*

I run down the stairs, down the hall and into the kitchen. The kitchen staff clear the room. They must sense my need to fill the gaping void with food. It will do me no good, but it doesn't matter.

I go for the fridge first. I bite into blocks of cheese, pies, and puddings. I guzzle milk like a baby calf–straight out of the container. The smell of a fresh chicken roasting draws me next...

I leave the kitchen a disaster.

Poof.

Feeling like a fat-ass, I lay in the grass in the dull sun to digest and plan. My stomach feels like it might explode. I stretch my arms and legs out like a star and take deep breaths, trying not to puke.

I wonder if this is where I landed after my battle with Lucifer? I wonder if my body left an indent when it crash landed and broke every bone? I was filled with fresh blood back then. I glance to Hellsky, nothing looks familiar from that night. I'm not sure if it would. I was high on adrenaline and blood and... love. Stupidly.

I am still for so long that a chickadee lands on my stomach and chirps. It pecks at my shirt, collecting the crumbs–probably from the pie–before flitting off.

I knew Sparrow wasn't the one the moment he stabbed me. How could you kill someone you love? We are not invincible together. At least he broke his family's curse. At least Thrush won't have to dedicate a portion of his life to being a Hellion like his uncle did.

I take a deep breath and unbutton my jeans.

"Jesus," Noah says, sitting cross-legged next to me. "Never thought I'd see the day that Meg nearly split her pants."

"It's bad. I know." I splay my arms and legs again.

"Are you waiting for the vultures to clean your bones?" Noah toys with a tall piece of grass, twisting it in his fingers.

"Maybe later." I close my eyes.

"Are we going to talk about the kitchen staff?"

"I said I was sorry."

"You scared them."

"I... I was... sad. Okay? Can they forgive me for being sad and trying to make myself happy by eating?"

"You ate *everything*."

I sigh. "I'll go on a diet tomorrow."

Noah chuckles. "Please don't do that. None of us need to deal with Meg on a diet."

"Remember that time we skipped school and stole that car and drove to Seabreeze?"

Noah settles next to me, his hands behind his head. "Yeah, Meg. Those were fun times."

"We got in a lot of trouble."

"Sure did."

"Look at us now."

"Look at you. I never thought the little girl who sat next to me in Kindergarten would turn into this."

"The ruler of Hell?"

"A pig." Noah laughs loudly at his own joke.

I slap his shoulder. "You're supposed to be my friend. You can't say crap like that to girls."

Noah holds his stomach, laughing.

---

oof. I'm standing in Jed and Shay's room. They're sleeping in the bed; Thrush is quiet in his crib. Noah is nowhere to be seen. That's good. I didn't want him to catch me in the act.

I do exactly what I told Noah I wouldn't do. I grab Thrush from his crib. Jed and Shay are shouting as I disappear with the baby. I find Gabriel next, his blue eyes wide as I interrupt him eating a ridiculously large plate of spaghetti and meatballs.

Poof.

We're standing beside the fountains of Babylon.

"This is the last place I expected you to take me." Gabriel looks severely disappointed as he wipes sauce off his face.

"Baptize him. Fast," I say.

Gabriel takes the baby from my arms. He whispers a prayer. Blesses his head and Thrush's. He dunks Thrush in the fountain, quick. Thrush waves his arms, startled and scratching at Gabriel. He lifts the boy, water dripping, his small mouth gasping for air. Gabriel chanting a prayer, a blessing, I'm not sure.

Thrush cries.

"Hurry," I urge.

Gabriel nods, praying faster.

He dips Thrush in the water again. It seems to be a long of a dunk. It's too long. The baby's arms stop moving.

Oh no. He's drowning Thrush.

"Stop!" I scream.

Gabriel's face twists, like he's fighting. "It's not me. I can't lift him."

"Get out!" I shout. "Get him out of the water."

"I'm trying," Gabriel says, but his whole-body jerks.

Once. Twice. He goes under, water splashing and running over the side of the fountain.

I run toward the fountain only to see a dark shadow under the water. Like a giant mouth, it swallows Thrush and Gabriel whole.

No. No. No. Noah is going to kill me. I can't go back home without the baby. The water of the fountain ripples, clear and blue as the sky. Whatever happened, there's no blood. That can only mean they're alive.

The Scarecrow once told me that water was a universal conduit. It could take us places. Move us between realms like the portals. I see it now. The fountain in the center of Babylon is nothing but a giant portal. To where? I'm not sure. But I don't wait to find out. I jump in after them.

Under the water I can hear it. The clicks and croaks and monotonous hollow song. Nothing like the songbirds from my windowsill. It's mournful, like a whale song in the ocean. *Plip-plop.*

Two Minutes to Midnight

Cool water soaks my clothing as I follow the shadow, and I hold my breath until my lungs feel like they'll explode. Going through the portal makes me feel sick. I kick and swim until I break the surface, gasping and choking.

It's night, the water dark like ink. Raindrops fall from Hellsky. I hear water splashing, a child crying, my father grumbling. I follow the noise, scrambling out of the water toward the shore, the moon my only light. I slip on wet leaves and mud.

There is a cabin in the woods with a dim light on the porch. Moonlight illuminates the muddy footprints and I follow them before they fill with rain water.

Croaks and clicks echo in the forest. The hollow song of the Nightjar fills my ears.

"Mine," a cryptic voice booms.

I see the light of Gabriel's blade.

I want to shout that I'm coming. But I want to be surprise help, not anticipated help. I don't want the

Nightjar to know I followed them. Wings would be good right now; I could fly over all these leaves and sticks littering the ground instead of sounding like a baby rhinoceros making its way through the woods.

Shouts from Gabriel make me abandon my attempts at being quiet. I run toward the cabin and shove my shoulder into the door. After three more shoves, it blasts open.

The scene in the cabin is something from a horror movie. I take a lot of life highlights from Shawshank Redemption, but this... this is something darker.

Thrush is floating in the air. His little face is panicked, silent tears rolling down his cheeks.

"Give him to me," Gabriel shouts, reaching.

"Mine," the cryptic voice hisses.

Demore looks like Dracula, changing forms from bird to giant winged shadow. A current of air circles the room, rustling the tendrils of her darkened form.

I grip my blade and stand next to Gabriel.

"Mine," it says.

"Are you Demore?" I ask.

"One should know their realm better," it replies. "You should know better than to steal my gift."

Thrush is quiet now as he watches, too afraid to cry or babble.

"He's not yours," I say.

"He's baptized," Gabriel says. "You're too late."

"Mine," it says. "My gift. They left it for me. My precious baby."

Gabriel signals with his eyes and the tip of his head.

We move together. Two steps for Gabriel to launch himself to Demore's height. It's four steps and a jump for me but I only make it a few feet in the air.

Demore screams, shrill and ear piercing. Thrush cries.

The wind in the cabin whips stronger. Dust and dried leaves take to the air. Demore reaches for Thrush, her tendrils of shadow wrapping around his tiny body. She is nothing but darkness now, a flowing void engulfing him.

"Mine," she says as she disappears through a hole in the roof.

Gabriel punches at the wood of the roof. Splinters of broken wood fall around him. He punches it harder, and harder, until blood drips from his knuckles.

"Stop," I beg. "Don't..." I press my lips together and run out the door to escape the blood and search for Demore's shadow amongst the darkened hellscape.

I see nothing, but I hear her call and the cries of the baby.

"This way!" I shout to Gabriel. "The voices are this way."

I run through the forest around lone sacks of walking flesh that wander aimlessly in the night. When the moon rises above the trees, they will sleep like the dead. They avoid me, but Gabriel is a different matter; their jaws snap at him and they turn to follow. But we are too fast, running with everything we've got, trying to find Demore and the baby.

"I don't see them," Gabriel says.

I slow my pace and tip my head, listening for the mournful call of Demore and the cries of Thrush.

There's nothing. Just silence.

"Damn," I mutter. "I can't hear anything."

Gabriel taps my shoulder and points to a clearing in the forest. Moonlight peeks from between the rain clouds and reflects off water like a mirror. There's a dark cloud, independent of the murky weather and lower to the ground.

We make our way to the pond, blades ready.

Something slithers beneath the surface; ripples disrupt the pond of glass on the far edge.

Gabriel pats my arm and points.

"Do we go in the water?" I ask.

"I'm going over it," Gabriel says as he takes to the sky.

I watch from the shore. Like a loser. No wings. No partaking. Just shivering in my damp clothes and dripping hair as the rain turns into a light mist.

The closer Gabriel gets, the farther away the dark cloud moves until it disappears.

Gabriel searches Hellsky before returning to the shore.

"They're gone," he says.

"Have you ever seen anything like that?" I ask.

"I heard stories, but I've never seen anything like that with my own eyes." He wipes at his mouth. "We must find Thrush."

"I know." I say.

———

"Tell me why I shouldn't trap you in the Astral for eternity," Noah is seething.

"You don't understa–"

"I told you to stay away from Thrush and you took him to another realm," Noah says.

Now, Noah's always been understanding. The best friend a girl could have. We've been through plenty together but this... this is something else(?). I'm not sure he'll ever forgive me.

"Why did you take him?" Shay asks.

"Yeah," Jed adds. "Didn't you do enough damage already?"

"I had to get him baptized." I point to Teari and

Gabriel. "He was going to turn into a Nightjar. I couldn't curse his entire life." I look to Noah. "You knew. You knew what fate held for him without the baptism. I couldn't let him turn into something else. Something like Elise. Don't you want more than a jar of feathers to mourn? Don't you want more for your son?"

There is silence. Most of the people in this room didn't know about Elise. They didn't know my unborn daughter died at the hands of the Hellions of before my rule. They didn't know she was a snowy owl who haunted the northern parts of Hellsky. She was two-thirds darkness and one-third light. She was the brightest light in the darkest places. She was the only child I'll ever have since that day I killed seven Hellions after they stormed my home and took more than just my spilled blood.

So I tell them.

I face Noah. "You're my best friend. You always have been. I couldn't let you go through what I did. That's why I took him to Babylon. I didn't know the fountain was a portal and Demore could get him. I didn't know." I reach for Noah, gripping his shoulders. "We are going to find him." I close my eyes and think of the jar of feathers on my nightstand. "If it's the last thing I ever do in this life, I will bring home your boy," I promise Noah.

The room is silent.

Guilt threatens to overtake me. They hate me. All of them. The flood of shame is overwhelming.

———

SKEELE

Skeele stood with Tukka and Chel and Klaus. They glanced to him as the scene unfolded. Meg was being thoroughly chastised by her friends and family. He was waiting to see what she was going to do next. Tensions were high and he was glad the new recruit Hellions weren't present. They'd feed on the tension; it would make them wild. They were having a hard enough time tampering down their rage with the bagged blood and saving their wrath for only when it was needed.

Noah and Meg's relationship was deep. Skeele wasn't going to get between them. Noah had told him stories of their childhood. And he was glad that the demon who raised her was dead, or he'd kill John Lewis himself. Meg had faced more pain than most. More deceit, more heartbreak. Skeele kept worse from her. He had his own secret. And when she found out that Skeele's father was one of the Hellions who'd raided her home on the Earthen plane, he was sure she'd kill him in an instant. She'd kill him just like she'd killed his father that night. Skeele didn't have Angel grace or a mixed blood to help his cause. He was Demon, through and through. The gene pool was small; the bloodline, even smaller. There was no separation from his father. It was the worst secret he could ever keep from her. Deep down he knew he was different. But he doubted that was enough to sway Meg's thoughts. She already hated him. Only used him for food. It wouldn't hurt her much to end him. She'd find someone else. There was no fairy tale ending for Skeele and he knew it. Still, it was better to be born of hate and die of sacrifice. That was more than most had accomplished in his position.

Meg

I go back to my room to shower and change into clothes better suited for hunting Hell-bound creatures. Tonight, we search for Demore and Thrush. I have a good feeling about it. I'm not sure if I've ever been more confident about finding someone. I'm going to find that baby if it's the last thing I do.

Noah hasn't brought me any food since I got back. I'm guessing it's his way of rebelling and hating on me. It's fine. I can survive. I survived a long while without his help. I'll do it again. But truthfully, I could really go for a Moons over My Hammy from Denny's. My stomach growls. I do my best to ignore it as I take a shower and try not to think about how Noah's tether to me is thinner than ever. I swallow down the fear that it might snap and break and I lose the best friend a girl could ever have. I lather with soap that smells like bergamot and lemon and scrub the mark on my thigh harder and harder, wishing it would rub off. The ouroboros reminds me that I always fuck up good situations. I am continuously threatened with resetting the balance. The ethereal equilibrium means so much to Babylon and the missing God of the Earthen plane and Hell. It actually doesn't mean much to me. From what I've seen, fuck resetting the balance. I think it's about time I embrace the chaos. I might have already. Or at least maybe the kitchen staff have embraced my chaos.

I change the bandage on my arm and inspect the cut that won't seem to heal. It burns from the soap getting into it. I dab at the redness before wrapping my upper arm with gauze and securing it with tape.

Standing in the closet I chose leather pants, ankle-high boots with a steel toe, and a dark blue shirt with a wide neck. I can't stand the thought of hair or clothing touching my neck right now. I pack my bag with a jacket, a small blanket, and clean socks.

I move through my room, rearranging and cleaning up. I stop at the jar of feathers on the nightstand. Picking it up, I tip the feathers and watch them fall.

"Help me find him, Elise," I say. I open the jar and take out one of the white feathers with few brown markings at the tip, the quill sharp and firm. I tuck it into my pocket.

The room cools. My breath becomes fog.

"What do you want, Clea?" I ask.

My mother appears in the center of my room. She's translucent with ruby red lips; pale and beautiful as always.

"You'll be careful," she says.

"Of course."

"Did you eat something?" she tips her head looking hopeful. "You'll need your strength, child."

"I'm fine." I adjust my bag and secure my blade to the thigh holster. "Were you going to tell me?"

"Tell you?"

"About Gabriel. You and Gabriel. I've been seeing you sneaking off and finding you together in dark rooms," I say. "Were you going to tell me that you've been seeing each other again?"

Clea smiles sweetly. "It's not like before. You see, I am a speck of what I once was." She reaches for me, touching my dark hair. "We weren't ready to say goodbye all those years ago."

"So, you're just saying goodbye?"

Her smile disappears. "Perhaps. Goodbyes can be long." Dismayed but calm, she closes her eyes like she's remembering. "Our time is finite. Ethereal beings or not, it's still finite. There are curses, dark magic, mortal wounds, our souls can get locked in the Astral. What we had was finite."

I nod, understanding. Every joyful moment I had lasted a second compared to other moments.

"Keep Teari and Shay safe," I make her promise.

She nods in promise, her image wavering and fading like a light bulb flickering out.

"Are you ready?" a voice asks from behind me.

I throw the bag over my shoulder and leave the room, following the giant shadow of Skeele as he walks through the halls quietly. His wings are tucked tight to his back, and I wonder if he's going to act like there's a stick up his ass this entire mission. I might have to snap his neck–or bite it. One or the other will do.

I press my hand to my aching stomach. I should eat. I should quell the thirst. Licking my lips, I watch Skeele walk. There isn't time.

We meet the others at the entrance to the burning caves. Chel, Klaus, Gabriel, and Jed are there. Noah appears, wavering. Shay was moved to the castle with Teari. They'll keep each other company while Clea and Tukka watch over them. The new recruits continue their duties with orders to notify Skeele if they hear the sounds of Demore in the night. She could be anywhere, but I doubt she'd go to the castle in the caves.

We go back to the pond where Gabriel and I last saw Thrush.

The Hellions go to the sky, a flock of dark figures.

"I'll carry you," Skeele offers. "It will be faster."

"No." I walk away from him toward Gabriel.

Gabriel can take me. I don't look at Skeele because I'm already too ashamed of myself for what I've done. Gabriel rarely judges my decisions, and he was there when Demore stole Thrush. I can't deal with the feelings from Skeele right now.

———

We land not far from where Gabriel and I left when Demore stole Thrush. The plan is to approach her cabin quietly and hope she doesn't disappear with the baby again. We will surprise her in our attack.

We walk in a scatter formation, taking up most of the road. Gabriel leads us to where we last saw Demore's cabin.

Skeele takes his place by my side. "I could hear your stomach growling from the Earthen plane."

I glare.

Skeele steps closer, very close. His upper arm rubs against my shoulder, and he tips his head to whisper in my ear so the others can't hear. "You know, it really hurts, Meg. You fuck me then kick me like a dog," Skeele says, his voice sounding rejected.

"Shut up."

"I know you're hungry." He shoves me a little with his shoulder, just harder than a nudge. "You don't have to ask. You can take."

"I said shut up."

The others have gotten a good distance away, following the cries of Demore. It wouldn't take long to catch up with them. They don't seem to care that I'm not with them. I look up at Skeele.

"Do you know how... humiliating it is to not be able to feed myself? To have to beg and hate myself afterward? The disgust. To have to force you to do it. And to feel..." I stop talking and start walking toward the group.

I've never been embarrassed about sex, but there's something about our relationship–what it was and what it's turned into–that makes my face hot. With others I've had no shame. But Skeele has always been so contained and strong and loyal to me, it feels wrong to use him like a happy meal. He sat by my bed twice now while I came back from the dead. No one has ever done that for me. All that time ago I woke alone in the hospital on the Earthen plane. I was alone when I came out of the coma. But here I wasn't alone. I always woke to Skeele watching over me. He deserves better.

With Sparrow it was different. We were wild and dumb. Young. Heck, we didn't even know who we were for half the relationship. I was stupid for thinking it could last forever.

Heavy footsteps behind me and a strong hand gripping my shoulder stops me from walking any further. Skeele pulls me backward, my back tight against his chest. Leathery wings surround us, providing privacy. The moonlight overhead illuminates his arms as they wrap around me. He cuts his left wrist with his blade and brings it to my mouth.

"Don't..." I start to say.

"Eat," he demands in my ear. "When we find Demore, you're going to need your strength."

I know what's going to happen the moment his blood touches my tongue. I straighten my spine, close my eyes, and tell myself to keep it under control.

"Eat," Skeele says but before he finishes, my hands slap against his arm, pressing the cut skin to my mouth.

Mmm. There is no road under my boots. No hunt. No group searching for Demore and the baby. There is me, and Skeele, his thick blood, his heat at my back, the rumble of

Hellspeak coming from his throat. I press my back against him as I drink, grinding my ass against his groin. I can't help it. It's what I do.

A thick arm wraps around my ribs and squeezes me tighter to him.

I drink.

The rumble of Hellspeak continues. Lips press to my shoulder.

I suck, the bloodlust burning me from the inside like a torch in the night.

Teeth press against my shoulder. I press my ass back harder. His arm grips me tighter. I want to go further. I want to shove his pants down, and mine, and fuck in the street unashamed.

But I don't do it.

I lick his arm until the sliced skin closes. I turn in his arms, hold up my own wrist and slice with the small blade from my waistband.

"No," Skeele says, a pained look on his face.

"You need your strength too," I say. "It's only fair. When we find Demore, I can't have you collapsing."

"I have the bagged blood."

"Not good enough," I say. "I don't know how you Hellions survive on that crap."

"It keeps the feral at bay," he says.

I press my wrist to his lips. "Then be feral tonight." I smile. "I give you permission to let loose."

He groans and looks away as I press my bleeding wrist to his lips. His mouth parts and I am thankful for his wings hiding us or the rest of the crew would be getting a good show right now. Skeele's lips press to the sensitive skin of my wrist and he draws. His gaze never breaks mine. Heat floods my lower stomach and I lean into him. One of his hands moves to my arm, holding it in place, while the other slides across my back and down, gripping my ass and pressing me harder against the bulge in his pants. I know that's not some obscure Hellion gear pressing into my belly. Of all the times I took what I wanted from him, I never thought it was because he wanted to or that something about me turned him on. Maybe I was wrong.

His eyes are dark as he stops, licks my wrist to seal the wound, grips me by the shoulders and pushes me back a few inches.

"Control," he growls. The blackness of his eyes shines.

"Are you telling me or yourself?" I ask.

He turns us before dropping his wings away and folding them behind his back. I straighten my clothes. I guess chivalry is not dead; in Hell at least.

Skeele motions for me to walk around him. As I pass, I glance down at his crotch. "You need some time alone with that thing?" I tease as I walk away and jog to catch up with the others. I don't miss his reply in Hellspeak that sounded like more cursing, and perhaps a threat.

———

A light rain mists the road. It smells like autumn, wet decaying leaves and a chill in the air.

"The pond is in that direction," Gabriel points at a heavily wooded area.

We see the lights of the cabin and make our way into the forest. The rain stops just as soon as it started and the lights of the cabin dim until they disappear.

We make it to the edge of the clearing where we all just saw the outline of the cabin, but it's gone.

"The cabin should be here," I say.

There's nothing but a break in the trees where the cabin should be. It looks like one of those paintings of a forest clearing with a backdrop of trees filtering the light.

The Hellions scope out the perimeter. Noah crosses the clearing, pausing to inspect the grass.

Plip-plop. The sound is faint.

"Demore is here," Jed says. "I can feel her."

I search the sky.

"This feeling has always saved me," Jed says before whispering a chant and crossing his arms to trace the runes on his skin.

I follow the sound. *Plip-plop.* It leads me to the pond we came through that night. Unfortunately, there is not a baby hovering over the center of it.

Noah disappears from the clearing and appears at my side. "Thrush is here. I think... we just can't see him."

Something moves in the water, disturbing the flat glass surface.

"When we saw the cabin, we had just come out of this water," I say. "We saw the cabin when it was raining a few moments ago."

"And?" Noah asks, moving to hover over the pond. "It doesn't seem special."

"A Scarecrow once told me that water was a conduit. We traveled through the water like a portal. I think we need to dunk ourselves to see it."

I walk into the pond as Jed tells Skeele. I go under the water until my hair is dripping and my clothing soaked, then I break the surface. Blinking a few times, I walk to the shore. The cabin is there, lights glowing from the windows. "Get in the water," I say. "I can see it. Water is a conduit to see it."

The Hellions and Gabriel move smoothly into the dark water.

"I'm not going in there," Jed says, standing his ground. "There's something wrong with that pond."

"Do what you gotta do, pal." I pat him on the shoulder and walk toward the cabin. The others follow, the cries of Demore becoming louder.

Through the windows we can see Thrush floating in the air, sleeping. Demore's viscous shadow circles the room. Her hollow notes and monotonous cries must've put him to sleep. I motion for someone to go to the roof, since that's how we lost her last time.

Skeele and Klaus fly to the roof, their boots landing gently. The shadow of Demore pauses its circling and changes shape into a ball around Thrush.

"Christ Almighty," Gabriel says. "She's getting ready to run again."

Plip-plop. Plip-plop. Plip-plop. Her hallowed call repeats faster and faster like a threat.

"I just hope we come out of this with our eyes." I step onto the porch, old wood creaking under my weight.

Demore weeps loudly. Thrush begins crying.

"Distract her," Gabriel says as he runs up the steps and blasts through the door.

I follow him, blade in hand. "Come here, Demore," I shout. "Come and get me."

Demore hisses. "Stupid." Tendrils of her shadow flow toward me. I chop at them with my blade.

Demore screeches. "He's my gift. My precious. My baby."

"He is not." I grab at her shadow-form but my fingers go right through her.

"I'll come for your eyes," Demore threatens. "All of yours."

The ceiling creaks before the Hellions break through. It must've collapsed under their weight.

Demore circles around Thrush and disappears through the giant hole in the roof.

"Mother of pearl," Gabriel runs out the door and takes to the sky. The Hellions follow.

Since I can't fly, I run.

Demore seems to be a creature of habit. She goes to the pond and suspends Thrush over it, just like before. Gabriel and the Hellions chase Demore across Hellsky. Noah hovers over the water, ready to catch Thrush when he falls.

Jed waits on the shoreline with me since neither of us can fly.

"This is ridiculous," Jed finally says. "Demore is playing with them." He watches Thrush hover over the water and Noah hover below him.

Jed crouches and empties his bag onto the sand at the water's edge.

"What are you doing?" I ask.

"I have an idea." He lays out a red square of cloth. "I've been reading up on this. I think it's going to work."

"I'm not sure this is the time for experiments," I say.

"They're not experiments," Jed sounds annoyed. "They've kept me alive this long."

He arranges bones and small black feathers on the square of cloth followed by vials of strange liquid and finally, a stick that he sets to smudge.

"What will this do?" I ask.

Jed points to the water. "You said that's a conduit?"

"Yeah." I nod.

"Then watch this." Jed chants strange words. His fingers dance in rhythmic and repetitive motions with the spell. The water in front of us bubbles softly. Steam rises. I look to

Jed and when I look back to the water a white, wispy form is taking shape.

"What is that?" I ask.

Jed simply chants louder and his fingers dance faster.

The form coming from the bubbles solidifies.

It's Nightingale.

———

"Night!" I start to move to her.

"Don't," Jed warns. "She's not here for you. I didn't call her for you."

I stop running toward her.

Nightingale looks just like the first day I met her: a black crop top and tiny red gym shorts with white piping-straight out of the eighties. She has headphones resting on her neck and she's wearing the big, clunky roller skates. She turns, her dark hair flowing down her back. She glides across the pond, skating. She twists and turns so fast her image is a blur. She whistles a melodic trill.

Noah turns away from Thrush.

It's hard to describe the moment Noah recognizes Nightingale. Everything changes. There's electricity in the air. The light from the moon dampers to a dreamlike haze.

Nightingale glides to Noah. She takes his hand and takes him into the air as though there is an invisible elevator. They circle as they rise until they are with Thrush.

Thrush floats between them and coos as he recognizes his mother. Nightingale whistles a gentle trill to Thrush before taking him into her arms and holding him close.

Plip-plop. Plip-plop. Plip-plop. Plip-plop. Demore comes from over the treetops, fast. Her mournful melody gets louder and louder.

"Mine," she cries out. "My precious. My baby. My gift." The dark shadow of the Nightjar soars faster to meet Nightingale.

Night holds out a hand. I'm not sure what she is but she has a power that stops Demore in her path. Nightingale's sweet, high-pitched chirping trills turn into guttural chatter that makes the hairs on my arms stand up straight.

"What are they doing?" I ask Jed.

He's standing at my shoulder, no longer chanting, and praying. "They're gonna fight."

Nightingale pushes Thrush into Noah's arms and then she illuminates, drawing all of the light from the moonlight until she's a giant, glowing orb. Demore's shadows grow and blacken, her tendrils draping the canopy of the forest.

I'm waving my hands at Noah, trying to get him to move back. Whatever they are doing, they are getting bigger and bigger and drawing energy from around them.

Gabriel sweeps down, white wings spread wide in all their glory, and grabs Noah and Thrush, bringing them to the opposite side of the pond.

Lightning crackles between the twisting balls of energy that Nightingale and Demore have become. They rise in the sky, swirling, crackling, screaming, and crying. Their forms shift and blur. They twist and jab. The wind picks up, blowing my hair out of my face until it's dry.

Without the water, I can't see Demore so good. I can't see her cabin. I step into the pond to soak myself again, submerging myself for a moment. My head breaks the surface. Nightingale sends a blast of light and electricity to Demore. The dark ball of energy shrinks and shudders in defeat.

The fight is over. Demore's cabin is dark. Her shadowed form roils behind the windows. Nightingale drops from

Hellsky like a ballerina, landing elegantly on one foot. She glides across the water on her roller skates, twisting and turning like an ice skater. She stops in front of Noah and bends to talk to Thrush. She says something to Gabriel and he takes to the sky, moving away.

I face Jed. "That was the best idea you've ever had," I say as I walk toward the shore. "You saved Thrush." Nothing can wipe the smile off my face.

Jed smiles and shrugs a little. "Nothing can defeat a mother's need to protect her child."

"It was per–" Something grabs my boot and jerks me backward. Hard. I drop, catching my upper body and grabbing handfuls of sand. Water splashes in my face. It jerks me backward again, harder. I go under in the deeper water. I splash, waving my arms, trying to scream only for my mouth to fill with water as I'm pulled under. I try to kick but my legs are immobilized, held tight together by something strong. It pulls me deeper and deeper until I can no longer see the light of the moon past the surface of the pond. Water fills my mouth as bubbles of the last bit of air in my lungs rises to the surface.

Darkness Calls, the Raven King

Skeele

"Where did she go?" Skeele shouted at the others. He flew closer, now that the battle was over, to find Gabriel. "She went under the water and never came out."

Gabriel frowned. "It's a portal. We went through it before."

"A portal to where?" Skeele asked.

"Babylon."

"No." Skeele shouted. He dove into the murky pond water, searching. He swam deeper and deeper until his lungs burned. He couldn't find anything. Nothing resembled a portal under the water. He broke the surface and chanted every portal opening phrase he'd come across. None worked. Nothing appeared under the surface.

Gabriel joined him.

Then Klaus.

"I can't find anything," Gabriel said as he broke the surface and caught his breath.

"Me either," Klaus said, spitting water.

Chel shook his head no.

Skeele's heart beat fast. He knew he didn't have much time. And goddamn him if his nightmares were going to come true today. He swam toward Gabriel, knowing he had enough of her blood to travel once. When he'd fed from her wrist at the start of the hunt, he hadn't taken much. He had one shot. Skeele grabbed Gabriel's shoulder and... *Poof.* Skeele and Gabriel went to Babylon.

MEG

I wake, coughing and spitting water from my lungs. It spreads across the cement floor I'm lying on, turning the gray dark. I cough hard, trying to get out all of the water. My chest aches, water drips from my clothes and hair.

There is a dark feather on the ground in front of me. A memory...

"...the last Argentavis feather ... "What did you show them, mother?" I whisper to the feather. There is an arc of static electricity, my fingertips tingle, my eyes widen and... I see... I see.

Wars. Blood and death. Good and evil. A dead Sparrow. A motherless child and a fatherless child. Light and dark. The earthen plane and the ethereal realms. A burst of bright light. An explosion. Fear and pain. Emptiness. A dark, never-ending vat of emptiness that would suck every joyful moment right out of me."

Sparrow had a vision that day too. Clea had given us both feathers.

"What did you see?" I demand. "Remember when I told you we're invincible together?" he asks. "Yes, and Clea said the

same thing." "I saw a dark future, one where we are separate."
He closes the space between us and takes my hand again. "She
showed me, Clea showed me."

I was afraid to lose the one person who had shown me
love and caring and truth. Whatever he saw, it wasn't worth
saving. Or maybe, it was exactly where we are today. Maybe
he didn't care to try and change our destiny.

The Raven King is waiting on the other side of the bars.
His dark wings are dripping with water. Those green eyes
damn me.

"That was really inspiring what you all did back there,"
Sparrow says. "Best part was seeing Thrush alive. And that
spell to bring Nightingale back." He slow claps. "Spectacu-
lar. The Archangels haven't seen magic like that in eons."

"Why didn't you just take what you wanted if you were
there?" I cough up water and move to my knees.

"Nightingale forbade it." He crosses his arms and looks
down at me. "I'm not going to mess with my sister. Especially in her Astral form. If I go after her baby, she'll put a
roller skate through my skull."

I sigh, relieved. "Then why am I here?"

"You killed that Deacon. They want retribution."
Sparrow makes a face. "There's something else they want
you to do. But they won't tell me what it is."

"I wish I had been the one to kill the Deacon. It was
Demore. His eyes were gone. He turned into a fast-zombie.
Someone injected Angel blood into him." I pause for
dramatic effect. "Who would have done that? We burned
the body." I hold my throbbing arm. "I'll kill every one of
them if you don't let me go."

Sparrow points to the opposite side of the cage. "It's
open. Remember when you and your filthy Hellion's cut
Gabriel out, the same passage is there for you."

I glance at the opening. It's a trick. It has to be.

The sounds of water splashing interrupts.

"Looks like we have a party," Sparrow says, focusing behind my cage.

I take the distraction as my moment to scramble out of the prison cell. I roll, pull myself up on aching legs, and climb through the hole in the bars. I hold on to the corner post, afraid of collapsing.

Turning, I see Skeele and Gabriel exit the fountain of Babylon. I've never thanked God before, but I consider it in this moment.

My chest hurts and ears ring from my near-drowning experience.

The other Archangels make themselves known from near Sparrow. Gabriel and the others exchange words. Wing beats resonate off the stone slab under our feet.

Skeele is at my side, soaking wet. Skeele's black eyes bore into mine. "Move," he says. "Be fast." He flattens his hand, lifts my leg, and puts my boot in his palm then throws me up into the sky.

My gut drops. I can't fly. What the hell is he thinking?

Sparrow drops like a hawk, blade drawn. I throw myself back and kick at his wrist. His blade goes flying. Michael comes next. No blade. He grabs my wrist and throws me higher into the air, laughing. I tumble, ass over teacup, in the air. My stomach threatens to empty itself. My arms and legs cycle. This fight has turned into a game of monkey in the middle; me being the monkey and not appreciating it one bit.

Sound like thunder and lightning erupts from the sky as Skeele, Gabriel, and the Archangels go at it with blades and swords.

Someone grabs me by the ankle. It's Michael. He throws me a hundred feet across the sky to Raguel.

Raguel grabs my wounded arm. I scream. I reach around with my good arm and grab onto his shirt. He tries to shake me off.

"You fuck," I seethe. I get a good grip and bite him on the hand.

He tries to shake me off, but I don't let go. I don't release my jaws until his blade comes out. I drop.

Poof. I climb Michael's back and bite him in the neck.

I nearly forgot the taste of Archangel blood and the power that comes with it. Maybe this is what Skeele meant when he said be fast. Eat fast.

Poof. I take it easy on Raphael out of respect for Teari. One bite on the neck. He collapses and falls to the ground. I wasn't expecting that. But it gives me an idea. *Poof.* I appear next to Raphael's body. I dig the snowy owl feather out of my pocket and collect the blood leaking from his neck into the hollow quill.

Gabriel lands near me, blade dripping with blood and out of breath.

Skeele lands next.

"She'll drain every one of you," Gabriel shouts at the Archangels.

Michael points. "She is filth. We are giving her to the Deacons."

Gabriel points his blade. I step in front of him and point my own blade. "You're not giving me to fucking anybody," I say. "I'll drain you dryer than the Sahara desert. Can your annoying ass live without blood? I don't think so."

Gabriel chuckles.

"You will leave me alone." I jab my blade at Michael.

"You will destroy that portal." I point to the fountain. "And if I sense you've been working with the Deacons, I'll drain you all." *Poof.* I grab Raguel by his neck and show my teeth. "I'm that fast." *Poof.* I return to Gabriel's side. "You will truce with Gabriel and allow him to return to his Kingdom."

"You don't know–" Sparrow starts to say.

"Shut up." I warn. "He was here before you." I drop my blade and secure it. My bandaged arm throbs and it's all I can do not to hold it and weep. "Let's go."

I walk away. Gabriel and Skeele follow, keeping the pace on each side of me.

Live, Laugh, Toaster Bath

MEG

"Are you coming back?" I ask Gabriel as we walk down the road to his Kingdom.

The last time I left Babylon headed in this direction it was in a Cadillac. Now, Heaven doesn't look much different than the Earthen plane. There's busted cars, rotting bodies on the sides of the road, chaos and destruction still lingering from the Fast-Zombie War.

Gabriel takes note of the broken gate to his home. "I'll have to get this fixed first," he says, testing the gates motion. It sags and scrapes the road.

"You think they'll leave you alone?" I ask.

Gabriel nods. "If they know what's good for them." He smirks with a finger held in the air. "Ah, it's good to have the largest Kingdom in the Seven Kingdoms of Heaven. I'll have this rebuilt in no time."

"But Sparrow said everyone was dead. The Legions are gone." I walk past the gate, eager to sit on the shaded, rambling front porch of my father's home since the sun of

Heaven is punishing me. I hold a hand over my eyes, wishing for sunglasses.

Gabriel laughs. "For Pete's sake, I'm a little smarter than your average Archangel. My Legion is fine and well. I hid them."

I scan his lands not noticing anything different or out of sorts. The house is there, giant and magnificent; the Legions barracks and training grounds down in the back, the walk-ways—although dingy—still in place.

I get closer to the house, remembering what he told me during the Fast-Zombie War when I came to find him. He did say he was bringing his people food and they'd be fine.

Skeele looks uneasy in this realm. I'm sure it feels about as far from home as he's ever been. He never gets more than ten steps away from me and keeps looking behind us and up to the sky. He flicks his wings every so often and I'm sure it's because he's sweating like a whore in church under this sun as well.

"I'm going to stay, Meg." He rests a giant, tattooed hand on the porch railing as I walk up the few steps and sit in the shade. "I'll be fine. Thanks for the hospitality in Hell." He reaches forward to shake my hand like a businessman.

"Any time you need to run from the law, Dad. I'm here for you." I press my palm to my throbbing upper arm.

Gabriel tips his chin at me. "You better get that looked at."

I rub my lower arm. "It's from Sparrow's blade," I explain. "He sliced me down to the bone."

"It hasn't healed?" Gabriel asks.

I shake my head.

"Hm." Gabriel rubs his scruffy beard, looking hard at the blood-stained bandage.

"Sparrow's you say?"

"Yea."

"You better have Teari look at that." Gabriel looks off in the distance. "You should probably go now. I'm eager to free my people from hiding."

"You don't want us to help you?" I tease.

"Not even a little bit." Gabriel doesn't attempt to move. He just stares me down like he really wants me to get the fuck off his land.

I guess I wouldn't want anyone to know where I hid my entire Kingdom of Angels either. Even though things are good between us today, I've seen families turn sour over something as minor as a curse. He can keep his secrets, I'll keep mine. Although Gabriel is my father, we might not always have such an amicable relationship. After all, he's been around for an epoch at least. And just like Teari said, people change. Just look at Sparrow. Look at me. I'd say look at Skeele but I sense he's always been halfway decent for a Hellion spawn.

"It was nice saving the realms with you," Gabriel slaps my back as I stand and move toward Skeele.

"I'd say 'anytime,' but nope."

I take Skeele's hand. From the shiver of his arm, I must've startled him. He spreads one leathery wing behind me like a shield.

Poof.

We return to a dark castle in the burning caves.

———

I push open the giant wooden door to the cave, weary but triumphant. In the dim light I notice Skeele's Hellion gear is marred and dented. No one gathers to greet us, other than the creatures that scurry and slither in the shadows of the castle.

"I think I need a shower." I pull my damp shirt away from my skin. After being soaked in pond water and then battling the Archangels, I'm sure I smell ripe. I consider inviting Skeele along for the shower but as we get closer to the Hellion lair, he strays further and further from my side.

He's probably tired of me using him like a Golden Corral buffet.

"Make sure you see Teari about that arm," Skeele says as he points to my bandage.

"I'm going to see her next." I pause and reach out. "Do you want to have dinner... or a dinner. With everyone?" I ask. "To celebrate."

Skeele smiles. It's small and a bit shy, maybe because he'd never expect me to invite him to something like that. His wings hang, tired and dirty. He tips his head toward the Hellion door. "Everyone would like that. It will raise spirits."

I smile a little too much and try to ignore the awkward tension in the hallway. But I'm coming down off a shit ton of adrenaline and it makes me stupid. "Okay. I'll see you later."

I walk toward the stairwell that leads to my room and try not to look back at the Hellion lair door.

I run into Clea on the stairs. She appears to be waiting, wringing her hands in worry.

"Hey," I say. "What's wrong?"

She was deep in thought and her image fades as she notices me. "Where's your father?"

"He's in his Kingdom. He stayed in Heaven."

"Oh..." Clea looks out the window. She's upset. "He didn't tell me he wasn't coming back."

"Maybe he didn't plan on staying?" I say.

"He left without saying goodbye," she says. "It's fine." She wipes at her eyes. "It's not the first time."

"I'm sure he'll be back. Probably sooner than we think."

Clea nods quietly as she fades into nothingness.

Twenty-six years later and he's still breaking her heart.

I walk up the last flight of stairs and down the hall to the room where Shay and Teari are. I knock twice before opening the door. It's empty. Uh oh. Dread floods me. Just when things were going so well.

Poof.

I go to the cemetery, relieved when I hear the giggles of Thrush from behind the fence. I grab the handle of the gate but it burns my hand.

"Ah!" I shout as I wave my hand, trying to cool the burning skin. "What the heck?"

"Meg?" Jed asks from the other side. "Is that you?"

"Yes it's me."

The gate opens.

"Oh, thank God. We thought you were gone." Jed opens the gate wide and lets me enter.

They're all there. Noah, Thrush, Nightingale, Shay and a handful of Hellions.

"You were supposed to be at the castle." I remind them.

"They were safe with me," Nightingale says. She's holding a sleeping Thrush and cooing to him and rocking him.

"Where's Teari?" I ask.

Noah nods toward the front door.

I pass Shay who's talking closely to a Hellion about survival gear and easy to hide weapons. "Welcome back," she says with a smile as I pass her.

I open the door to the chapel and find Teari sitting in a chair and staring at the wall.

"How's it going?" I ask, closing the door and sitting next to her.

"What do you want, Meg?" Teari seems suspicious.

I lean back and pull the snowy owl feather out of my pocket. "I have something for you. Something that I think will help."

Teari holds up her nubbed arms. She clicks the hooks of the prostheses. "These puppies help me more and more every day."

"Then why are you sitting in here alone?"

She makes a face. "It's hard seeing Nightingale like she is."

"At least we get more time."

"True," Teari says. She notices the feather in my hand. "What's that?"

I grab her arm, pull it straight, and stab the quill into her soft skin.

"Meg!" Teari screams. "What are you doing?"

The quill empties of Raphael's blood and I set the feather on her lap. Teari's face turns red. She knocks off the prostheses, leans back on the couch, and holds up her nubs crossed on her chest. Slowly, her arms start growing. There's a commotion in the room as Jed and Shay and a few Hellions shove open the door.

"I knew we couldn't trust you in here. What did you do?" Jed asks me.

"Oh, just performing a miracle," I say. "But I'm hurt, really. Why must you always assume the worst of me?"

Jed walks over to Teari as her arms elongate into hands and fingers.

"I always assume you're up to some shit," Jed says. "But this is better than I was anticipating." He jabs me in the shoulder, playfully.

I fake a yawn and rub my arm, holding in a wince.

Teari's fingers have grown back. She waves her hands in front of her face, disbelieving.

"Oh my God," Teari exclaims as she stands. "This is the best." She runs toward me, throwing her arms around my neck and hugging me too tightly. "Thank you, Meg."

"It was nothing." I pat her back awkwardly.

She pushes me away, wrinkling her nose. "You stink."

———

SKEELE

Skeele stood at the wooden, lacquered bar and ripped open the bag of cold blood. He drank the entire bag without stopping to take a breath, then reached for another.

"Don't choke on that," Klaus said with his eyebrows raised in concern.

Skeele had been back for a few hours but had barely spoken. It was clear that he'd been fighting, but he had yet to tell them who he fought or who won. They could smell the air of Heaven that clung to his clothes, so they had a few clues.

"I can empty the fridge," Tukka offered, his dark red skin reflecting off the glass door as he opened the fridge again. "We can restock."

Skeele simply shook his head in agreement.

Chel appeared from the shadows in the corner of the room. He grabbed a glass tumbler from under the bar and a bottle of whiskey. He poured the whiskey into the glass– more than a shot–and slid it across the bar to Skeele.

Skeele dropped the bag of blood, picked up the glass, and downed it in one swallow. He waved for Chel to keep them coming.

For a good thirty minutes Skeele alternated between drinking the blood and the whiskey. Tukka, Chel, and Klaus were starting to get concerned.

"Where are the new recruits?" Skeele finally asked.

"Some are in the barracks, sleeping," Klaus said.

"Half are on assigned rounds," Tukka said.

Skeele shook his head in satisfaction.

He finally sat in one of the barstools and slowed his rate of ingesting the whiskey and blood. The others stayed close, worried.

Skeele told them about the battle with the Archangels. He rubbed his face and horns. "I've been dreaming that she dies in Babylon," he said. "I thought this was the day."

"We won't let that happen, boss," Tukka said.

Skeele nodded in agreement. He'd do everything in his power to prevent it, but he couldn't get the image of Meg on the ground in that cage out of his head.

"Is there more?" Chel asked quietly.

Skeele nodded and cleared his throat.

Skeele's blade clashed against Michael's. He wasn't prepared to take on an Archangel alone. Michael shoved and kicked. Raguel fought dirty, ripping Skeele's wings from behind. Skeele roared in pain before kicking Raguel in the chest, sending him backward. Fighting in the air was unfamiliar to Skeele. Gabriel came to his rescue one too many times. He had started to feel like a burden in this battle. He had started to feel like they were going to lose. Worse, he watched the Angels toss Meg through the air like a doll. It took her too long to get her bearings and use her power.

The Angels had said things to him as they fought. Dirty pig, Disgusting Hellion, wretched dog. If Skeele was ever considered a skilled protector, the Archangels were more skilled at spewing sinful language from their tongues. It grated on his conscience. The words they used weren't that far from Meg's language when she said she hated the Hellions.

Skeele was starting to wonder if maybe his father's kind of Hellion was better equipped. Hellions from Lucifer's rule weren't swayed by the foul talk, they'd give it right back and then some and follow up with violence. But the old Sparrow had taught Skeele to be different. Skeele had studied human and Angel ways. Humanity and angelology had become a part of him and as much as he hid it, he was struggling at the moment with the clash of emotions swelling inside him. His brain was running a thousand miles an hour processing everything that had just happened.

He was quite sure he could have handled it all just fine if Sparrow hadn't whispered to him when their blades clashed together. *"Don't you hear that heartbeat? That's mine. And I will take it."*

Now Skeele was on edge. He couldn't hear heartbeats from far away. It was just another threat.

Worse was the way he flew into the pond to find Meg. He couldn't get over it. He risked everything. His whole life.

And the worst part was, she'd never know how much she meant to him. She'd only know him as a warm bag of blood and a disgusting Hellion.

Amidst the ruins of their battlefield in Babylon, Skeele stood alone. The echoes of the clash between the forces of Heaven and Hell still reverberated in his mind, but his thoughts were consumed by a different torment—one that cut deeper than any sword. Skeele's bloodline was known for being ruthless and cunning. Yet, his heart, blackened by darkness, burned for Meg.

He watched Meg and Gabriel, his eyes clouded with a mix of longing and bitterness. He had fought alongside Archangels and the leader of Hell. He'd hoped that his valor would change her view of him. But despite his efforts, Meg's heart remained distant, unyielding.

The weight of his unrequited love pressed upon Skeele like an invisible burden. He had watched Meg's attention and affection bestowed upon her friends and family, their mere existence eroding his spirit. Every smile she directed at another, every whisper of endearment he overheard, chipped away at the fragments of his shattering soul.

Skeele understood the futility of his desires. He knew Meg was not one to be possessed or tamed. Her heart was a tempest, feral and wild, resisting the constraints of any suitor, including him—the commander of her fearsome legion of Hellions.

His thoughts were interrupted by the sound of Tukka cleaning up the bartop. The war may be won today, but his internal struggle, his battle for Meg's heart, seemed an endless cycle of torment. She was obsessed with a man who tried to kill her and the fact that Sparrow's heart still beat was competition.

With a heavy heart, Skeele summoned his strength and

resolved to set aside his personal anguish. There were battles yet to be fought, Hellions to command, and the leader of Hell to serve–without getting attached. He would carry on, his affection forever unreturned, but his loyalty to Meg unwavering.

Skeele stood from his seat and made his way to his room. As he took his first step forward, he promised a vow. He would be the fiercest warrior Hell had ever seen, not for the promise of love, but as an offering to the throne.

———

MEG

Teari inspects the cut on my arm. "It hasn't healed, even with fresh blood?"

"Nope," I say, wincing.

"This is easy. I've seen this before. Sparrow's blade must've been dipped in poison." She makes a face.

"You outdid yourself, Meg." Teari says. "I didn't need hands for this."

She calls for Noah. "Go get the baby basilisk."

Noah leaves, returning a few moments later with a covered wicker basket. He's making a face. "It's bad enough you make me feed these things," Noah says. "I don't like handling them."

"Be nicer, Noah," I say. "They lost their mom. She gave her life to the Seven Kingdoms of Heaven."

"Do they want the rest?" Noah deadpans.

"Stop arguing," Teari scolds as she pulls the basket closer, opens it and reaches inside. "These things are so slimy," Teari complains. The baby basilisk writhes in her hands, slime dripping on the floor. It stops moving when she places it near my arm.

The baby basilisk opens its mouth in anticipation, and she moves it closer until it latches onto the skin surrounding my wound. "It's like on the Earthen plane, with the leech therapy. The basilisk sucks the poison out."

I shiver. "Gross."

"They're good creatures to have around," Teari says. "We don't have them in the Seven Kingdoms of Heaven. Or the Earthen plane. The doctors at that hospital told me about the leeches, they've got to be the closest thing that resembles these there." Teari pets the basilisk. It breaks suction and twitches. Teari settles the creature in the basket before inspecting my arm again. "I think it got the poison out." She cleans my arm and wraps it in white gauze. "If this doesn't heal in a few days, you'll need to have the basilisk drain it again."

"Wonderful." I'd prefer a puppy or a kitten to the slimy basilisk.

———

MEG

Noah talked me into wearing a dress. It's low cut and tight and smooth against my skin. I've worn less so I'm not sure why I feel so uncomfortable.

Clea suggested opening the exterior doors so we can see Hellsky while we celebrate. It's a clear night with an infinite spattering of stars and a full moon.

I stare at Skeele who is standing in front of me, ready to open the door. He's wearing some kind of formal wear that's black and gray. He looks really good, even with the scruff on his face and the dark circles under his eyes.

"You ready?" he asks, one hand on the door.

"I think so," I say, smoothing my hands over the black satin dress. "Is this too much?" I ask.

Skeele focuses on the feather in my hair, then looks away and pushes the door open. "You look good," he says quietly. "The others will be pleased your ass isn't hanging out."

The formal ballroom is huge, with tiled floors and cavernous ceilings. Giant open archways let in the moonlight. The room seems too big for the dozen or so people who came. There are three tables in the center of the room. The pizza and drinks are off to the side. Another table has a record player set up and Nightingale glides over to change the song.

Noah appears at my side. "Meg," he smiles, "You're looking much better than the trailer park I pulled you out of."

I slap at his shoulder. "Just wait, a few drinks and you'll be wishing you left me back there. You can take the girl out of the trailer park but not the trailer park out of the girl."

I walk to the food table and get a plate with three slices of pizza and a mug of the spiked punch. I sit next to Teari as she's explaining the healing benefits of the basilisk to Tukka and Chel.

Everyone is lighthearted and chatting. There's no doom of impending Archangel fights. No threats from the Deacons. No chomping of fast-zombie jaws.

I eat the pizza and down the punch.

Nightingale dances with Thrush on her hip and Noah in front of her. The record player is blasting *Take On Me*. Thrush jabbers and moves his arms in what I can only imagine is baby dancing.

I Wanna Dance With Somebody comes on. The urge to dance is strong and Klaus must notice.

"Would you like to dance, my Queen?" Klaus asks with a bow and his palm out. He's wearing a purple button down and black slacks. His sleeves are rolled up, and it appears he's been cutting-a-rug for some time now.

I slap my hand in his and let him pull me to my feet. He drags me to the section of the ballroom where Noah and Night are dancing. Tukka dances alone until Clea shows up. I bust out every move I learned in Gouverneur elementary school and let the music take me back to a simpler time. I forget about basilisk and Nightjars and Scarecrows and Deacons. I let them evaporate from my mind and revel in the feeling of a full belly and warm night and clothes that fit and a day without a fight. I focus on that feeling of snow at Christmas and the hope of New Years Eve, Cadbury Eggs stolen from the local gas station because I wasn't getting an Easter basket from my fake dad. You know, simple feelings from simple times. Nostalgia stings realizing you can never go back, you can only remember that feeling. You can never go back home, you can only create a new home and better memories.

Klaus takes my hand and spins me, he pulls me close before dipping me and spinning me again.

"I didn't know Hellions could dance," I say, out of breath.

"We can do plenty of things," Klaus says. "Dancing is just the tip of the iceberg."

Time of My Life starts playing.

"Oh my god," I say. "I haven't heard this song in a million years."

"On day you'll say that, and it will be accurate," Klaus jokes.

"Do you know the dance from the movie?" I ask.

He makes a maybe motion with his hands but the smile on his face tells me he knows. Klaus takes both my hands and soon we are mimicking *Dirty Dancing*. I'm Jennifer Gray and he's Patrick Swayze and nothing matters but getting the final move just right. My dress isn't the right fit for all the twists and turns but I hitch it up so I can bend my knees better. Klaus doesn't get too close, but he does all the lifts and spins like this old movie from the eighties is his lifestyle.

"Are we doing the lift?" he asks.

"If you can lift me," I say backing up. I probably don't back up far enough, but I run at him and he swings me up into the air. My stomach flip-flops as the memory of being tossed by the Archangels hits. I push it away and plaster a smile on my face. My friends don't need to deal with my baggage tonight. I don't want to deal with my baggage tonight.

Klaus sets me on my feet and we laugh.

"You did it," he says, his expression so joyful he's almost handsome.

I curtsey like I grew up in a castle or went to a Miss Manners class as a kid. We all know better though. I learned how to curtsey from watching actors do it on TV. This is only the fourth time in my life I've ever curtsied.

The song fades and *Every Breath You Take* starts playing. Klaus gives me a questioning look. He knows I can't handle too much of the touching. I spin away from him with a promise to dance to something with a faster beat in a few minutes.

I make my way to the balcony and get a look at the stars. Skeele is there, hiding in the shadows. Lurking, and if I didn't know better, sulking.

"I thought you were Chel," I say, "He's usually the one lurking in the shadows."

Skeele tips his head but doesn't speak.

"Do you want to dance?" I ask, walking toward him.

"The song's almost over," he shakes his head but doesn't move away.

I pause, my confidence wavering. After all we've been through, the rejection throws me for a loop. I wanted us to have one night of fun, one night of relaxation. No rules, no wars, no realms, or rules.

Time After Time starts playing.

Something changes in Skeele's eyes.

Maybe he sees how his rejection hurt.

He reaches out with both arms, grips my elbows, and brings me to him. "What's wrong?" he asks. "Are you hungry?"

"No." I smooth my hands up his arms and consider telling him yes. "I asked if you wanted to dance." I search his face for an inkling of what he's thinking. He is stone. A statue. Unreadable. I sway to the slow song.

It takes a minute for Skeele to loosen up and move his hands to my hips. Maybe it's because all of our intimate moments have been in my room. Never in public.

"I never thanked you for coming to save me in Babylon," I say.

Skeele moves us back into the shadows so no one in the ballroom can see us.

"I will follow you to Babylon, to Hellsky, to the ends of the Earthen plane," he promises as he tips his head and touches his lips to my bare shoulder.

"Thank you–"

Poof.

Skeele is gone.

I step to the doorway and notice his figure in the shadows on the other side of the ballroom.

Damn, that stings.

Pour Some Sugar On Me starts playing and Nightingale whoops. She's dancing with Klaus and Noah is dancing around the room with Thrush as he giggles and drools all over his father's shirt.

Clea is laughing at Noah's dance moves and clapping her hands along to the beat of the song.

Poof.

I move to Clea's side. Her cold hand touches my elbow. "Thrush is adorable."

I nod in agreement, swiping at my hair to move it out of my face. My fingers touch the feather in my hair. The realization hits me that I will never have a moment like this of my own. I will never dance my own child across the ballroom floor because mine is lost, gone, nothing but a jar of feathers sitting on my nightstand.

Suddenly I feel ill. The three pieces of pizza and spiked punch crawl back up my throat. Maybe I should have eaten a little slower. I start walking for the door fast, not wanting to ruin everyone's evening with my vomit.

I move faster, then run.

"Meg?" Teari calls from behind me.

I open the first door I come to and thank the stars when I enter an empty room with a trash bin.

I puke up the pizza.

Teari is handing me a napkin. Tears sting my eyes as I hear baby Thrush giggling from the ballroom.

I pause. It still hurts, knowing that motherhood will never be for me. My womb is gone. Cut from–

"When Teari healed you, she healed all of you. Even what you lost."

Oh shit.

"Teari," I ask quietly. "I have never had a period since I transformed."

She looks at me, questioning.

"When you healed me, a long time ago. You healed all of me." I blink hard at her, annoyed that she's not understanding. "Like my fucking womb. Teari, give me some details."

"Angels and Demons and what you are, we don't have periods." She clears her throat. "Do you miss that?"

"Absolutely not." I lean closer to her. "Why don't we have periods?"

"It's just the way it is." She closes the door and sits next to me. "Something to do with the immortality."

Okay. Okay. This could just be a stomach bug or bad cheese or anxiety. A year without a period... some women would kill for that. I should be thankful, exuberant. I should be rolling in my bed like Scrooge McDuck with all the money I've saved not buying feminine products.

"Why are you asking?" Teari touches my back. Her hand slides down my spine, pausing at my hips. Her eyes widen. "Oh..."

"Don't say it," I warn her.

"Meg." She stands and paces the room. "Meg, who's..."

I close my eyes and curse every decision I've ever made. "Get rid of it," I beg. "Please, Teari. Get rid of it."

Her hands raise in defense. "I can't."

"You can!" I stand. "You can and you have to." A bout of nausea forces me to sit again and take deep breaths. "Please take it away. I don't want it. Not like this. Not under these circumstances. Make it go away."

Teari touches the feather in my hair. "Maybe this is a good thing. Maybe it's what we all need."

"I don't need this." I shake my head and swallow down

the giant lump of emotion in my throat.

She tries to calm me. "You've been through some rough shit, Meg. But it's going to be ok. This is... this is a miracle. Thrush was the first baby born in nearly a century."

I grab her arm. "It's not a miracle, Teari. This isn't Sparrow's." I stare into her eyes, ready to puke and scream and poof to the moon.

"Then who..." her hands fly to her mouth. "Oh Lord."

"You all did this to me." I point at her. "You made me use him for food. You and Noah." I hold back tears. This is the worst news in all of my life. "Why the fuck did you make me use a Hellion?"

"We didn't force you to fuck him, Meg." Teari says quietly. "We wanted you to eat. You were not well. We couldn't watch you go on like that."

I slap my palms together. "They go hand in hand. Do I need to write a book on it? The blood eating leads to the bloodlust. I drink the blood, I fuck anything with legs. I didn't make these rules. It's just the way it is."

Teari grabs my hands and holds them together. "This is a miracle Meg, whether you see it or not. It's a miracle." She blesses herself, like I'd expect an Angel to do. "I won't help you get rid of it. I can't. I'll do everything I can for you. But there's a heartbeat in your womb and I won't make it silent." She clears her throat. "You have time to figure this out. A Demon's gestation is much longer than an Angel's. There's time to make things right."

"How much time?" I ask, wondering how long I'll have to live like this.

"Usually about eighteen months or so."

Tears pour out of my eyes. I lean forward and heave onto the floor. After what happened to me and Elise, I can't do this again. I can't.

Promises, promises

Meg

I wait until everyone goes to bed before going back to the ballroom. I change into jeans and a T-shirt and steal some bagged blood from the Hellion's lair.

My bare feet fall softly on the tile floor of the Ballroom. I veer away from the pizza and punch. There's empty plates and glasses at the tables. Confetti and napkins litter the dance floor. I tuck my hands in my pockets and pad to the record player.

It's on, the black ring in the center circling, static playing in an undulating hum. I flip through the records on the table and select *Time After Time*. It's been a long time since I listened to this on repeat and got lost in a mood. I set the record on the player and settle the needle. The record spins and the song starts. I bob my head to the beat, turn away from the table, and head for the balcony.

I grip the railing, take in a deep breath, and lean over the edge to look down. The railing presses into my stomach.

"You're not going to jump, are you?" Skeele's voice asks.

I turn to face him. "Not tonight. But, I can't promise about tomorrow."

He frowns. "Don't say that."

"Fine. I won't jump. Not until I get my wings." I cross my arms and turn again. My hand rubs the bandage on my arm.

"Does it hurt?" Skeele asks, focusing on the injury.

"A little."

Skeele grips my hips and turns me to face him. His eyes search my face. "Just a little?" he questions.

"It's fine."

He tugs me closer. "Are you hungry?" he tips his head, revealing the thick, pulsing veins in his neck.

I lick my lips. I'm hungry, but I'm not going to tell him. I'm trying to wean myself off him, I started the moment he refused to dance with me. My ego is too hurt.

"What's wrong?" he asks.

"I just wanted to dance."

His lips part. "You danced with everyone in the room."

"Except you."

"Is that all you want?"

"Yes."

The song repeats in the ballroom. The soft crescendo of the keyboard gets drowned out by the clock ticking percussion sounds. *Lub.... Lub-dub.* It's like a heartbeat.

"Okay," he says quietly as he holds me tighter. His dark wings spread, he steps up onto the balcony railing, carrying me, and jumps off. Skeele beats his wings, raising us higher into Hellsky.

He holds me tighter than anyone ever has, his face buried in my neck, the music playing in the background. I wrap my arms around his waist and tuck my hands into his back pockets. He spins and rocks us to the beat of the song.

For a moment I forget that his child is growing in my belly. I ignore the fact that he should know. He doesn't need this burden. He barely tolerates me most days. And no one should have to handle the baggage that I bring to this party.

Time after time I keep making the same mistakes. The same stupid decisions. Living with my heart and not my head. Not this time. This time I'm going to do it differently.

What Skeele doesn't know won't hurt him. He'll finally be freed of me. He can have his life back. Heck, I never asked him if he had a girlfriend before I took him to my bed. I'm not going to be selfish this time. I'm going to be cognizant and compassionate and better than I used to be.

The End

About the Author

M. R. Pritchard writes about the elemental struggle between good and evil, and gods and monsters, and about people who turn into gods and monsters. Usually with a mix of apocalypse or post-apocalyptic setting. She also includes a spec of a love story because what is humanity without love?

M. R. Pritchard is a two-time Kindle Scout winning author, her short story "Glitch" has been featured in the 2017 winter edition of THE FIRST LINE literary journal, and her short story "Moon Lord" has been featured in Chronicle Worlds: Half Way Home (Part of the Future Chronicles).

M. R. Pritchard holds degrees in Biochemistry and Nursing. She is a northern New Yorker transplanted to the Gulf Coast of Florida who enjoys coffee, mint chocolate, cloudy days, and reading on the lanai.

Visit her website MRPritchard.com and sign up for her newsletter. You'll get a monthly newsletter with updates, day to day shenanigans, and book deals.

Sparrow Man Series/Rebranded as VEIL OF SHADOWS Series

Thread the Bone

Fantasy/Fairy Tale Love Story/Romance:

Muse

Forgotten Princess Duology

Midsummer Night's Dream: A Game of Thrones

Poetry/Short Story Collection

Consequence of Gravity

Preview of Night Owl (Book 6) - unedited

Turned to Gray

Meg

The warm body next to me shifts. Dragging the sheet. I open my eyes. It's Skeele. Of course, it's Skeele. It wouldn't be anyone else. He didn't leave after I fed. He was probably too tired. It's been weeks since dinner in the ballroom and things have been off between us. Not that they were ever really going well. He's still grumpy but does whatever I tell him. Every time I need him, he's there.

The aroma of coffee fills the room as a breeze blows through the open balcony doors. Noah left coffee and donuts. Not long ago I loved the smell. But today, it causes my stomach to lurch. I slide out of the bed and run to the bathroom.

"What?" Skeele asks, sitting up quickly, ready to fight.

I wave as I run, slam the bathroom door, lock it, and dry heave into the sink since there's no food in my stomach to puke up. I turn the water on high to hide the sounds. I don't want him to know. I don't want him to ask. From the corner of my eye, I watch the doorhandle to see if it moves, to see if he tries to follow me in here. I don't want to be caught purging my hopes and dreams into the sink.

It's nothing, I tell myself. *Just ate some bad burritos.* Burritos are never really bad though. I watch my distorted reflection in the sink plug. It could be worse. I could be broke and homeless and living on the Earthen plane. Yeah, that's it. I could be stuck never knowing that I was more than just a trailer-park girl in a small-town fighting tooth and nail to live the American dream. I grab a towel and wipe my face. Look at me now.

I lean against the counter and press my face into the towel. *Look at me now.* I have fluffy towels, a real bed, a kitchen with food, clothes that I didn't have to steal. Squeezing my cheeks, I swallow down the lump that's rising in my throat.

*

Skeele

Skeele opened his eyes and lay still, listening to the sounds of Meg retching in the bathroom. Gnawing doubt and torment clawed at his heart. He gave himself to Meg, gave his body and his blood but he couldn't shake the persistent feeling that she despised him. She'd said it to his face enough times. His mind spun with uncertainty. The time they'd spent together in darkest hours of the night seemed like a cruel illusion, tormenting him with false hope. He was sinking into a pit of self-doubt and despair. It had been hard to shake after his fight with the Archangels. He couldn't shake their words.

Dirty pig, Disgusting Hellion, retched dog.

Skeele stood and straightened the blankets. He collected his clothes, pausing to catch his reflection in the mirror. Shadows crossed his face. *I have pledged my life to her,* he thought, *why does she despise me? I make her physically ill. She can't even look at me.*

Skeele dressed quickly and left the room.

He walked through the halls of the castle within the burning caves. The pain of rejection would serve as fuel, he would remain loyal, a relentless warrior, a commander of unparalleled strength. He would ensure Meg's reign would be unchallenged, her enemies crushed. She could hate him, but he would forever remain loyal and serve. It was in his bloodline, his fate forever solidified in the stars of Hellsky. Meg could use him, that's what he was born and bred for. Serve the throne, nothing more.

Skeele was dizzy, his throat becoming drier with each step. He felt like he hadn't eaten in weeks. He tugged at the waist of his pants. They were looser than ever. He had fed Meg, but didn't take from her like before. Something internal warned him not to. He couldn't place the feeling, but he sensed she needed all the blood for herself. That wound on her arm wasn't healing and Skeele didn't want to risk her not being in full health.

He took one step down the winding stairs that led to the Hellion lair, on the second step, something strange happened to his body. The fog in his brain intensified, he stumbled and fell. Skeele rolled down the stairs like a tossed manikin. He finally stopped at the first landing where the stairwell turned sharply. Dark red blood dripped into his eye but he didn't care much because he was passed out.